No Words in English

No Words in English
A NOVEL

Elizabeth Kouhi

NORTH STAR PRESS OF ST. CLOUD, INC.

Cover design: Cecelia S. Dwyer

ISBN: 0-87839-135-5

Printed in the Unites States of America by
Versa Press, Inc., East Peoria, Illinois.

Published by:
North Star Press of St. Cloud, Inc.
P.O. Box 451
St. Cloud, MN 56302

Chapter One

The family was going deeper and deeper into the woods. The sun was already hidden behind the trees and the road was turning shadowy. Anna leaned over the edge of the wagon to peer ahead, but she could only see more woods. *How long before we get to our new home?* she wanted to ask Father, but he was sitting on a seat in the front with Mother, while Anna and her sister, Liisa, were on the floor at the back of the wagon surrounded by bags and suitcases. He wouldn't be able to hear her over the rattling of the wagon wheels. Anna shivered and pulled her coat closer. She glanced at her sister, but Liisa still looked angry. Anna didn't dare talk to her.

Anna had never seen such big woods before, even though she was used to wooded roads. The road to Mummo's from the town of Kotka, where they had lived in Finland was a road through the woods, but this was different. So far, Anna had seen only a few cabins in small clearings, rather than the fields and villages of her old home. The woods too, were different. Somehow these seemed thicker. The underbrush and small trees growing under the bigger ones made a wall that was just beginning to green.

How far, how far? repeated inside her head. She tried to settle herself more comfortably against the bags.

Anna's father had come to Canada two years earlier. He had worked in a mine to earn enough money to buy a stove, nails, some lumber, and other things necessary for starting a new homestead. Work in pulpwood camps during the past winter had earned him enough to buy tickets for their passage to Canada and money for food along the way. He had also bought a cow and a few chickens.

Anna had been excited by all the preparations after Father's letter came with the tickets, but Liisa, who was five years older, protested bitterly.

"What's the matter with you, you've known all along that we planned to go to Canada when Father sent for us," Mother scolded.

Nothing would change Liisa's mind. She hated leaving their home in Kotka and she was desolate at leaving her friends. She refused to take any interest in the new things along the way that excited Anna—the first big ship on the North Sea, the big horses in Hull, the noise and the crowds in Liverpool, and the even bigger ocean ship that took many days to cross the Atlantic. When the ship docked at Quebec City, she wouldn't come out of her sulks. And now, after the long train ride, she was like a thunder cloud. It was no use talking to her.

The steady rhythmic jolting of the wagon finally put Anna to sleep. When she woke, the wagon had stopped and it was nearly dark. Liisa was gone from her side and she could hear Mother's and Father's voices somewhere in the distance. When she tried to sit up, she realized that Father's big coat was over her. Just as she began to scramble to her feet, Father came out of the little log cabin.

"Well, my girl, we are home, we are home, our very own home. It's not much yet. In fact, it's only a sauna dressing room. I was too busy with the other buildings—the barn and the chick-

2

en coop. We had to have those first to have food, milk, and eggs—and of course we had to have a sauna. But I'll build a house for us this summer," Father explained as he lifted Anna off the wagon.

Anna looked at the cabin. It was just like the sauna on Mummo's farm except that the logs looked much newer. She could see yellow lamplight glowing from the little windows and the open doorway.

"Your mother is fixing up a bed for you and Liisa in the two cots I made for you. You can go right to sleep after you have eaten. It's very late. A neighbor brought some food for us because she knew we would all be tired. Tomorrow you can run around and explore your new home," said Father.

The sauna dressing room didn't look like a dressing room to Anna. Instead, it looked like a mixture of a kitchen and bedroom, with a table, stove, cupboard, a bed, and two benches. Two cots of canvas and wood leaned up against the far wall. There were familiar home-woven mats on the floor. Only the door into the sauna at the other end showed that it was a sauna dressing room.

"I'll just carry the bags in and then take the horse and wagon back to Korpi's. I won't be long. You get settled for the night. Tomorrow we'll start our new life in our new home."

Liisa was about to say something but Mother gave her a warning look.

Anna was almost too tired to eat but once she started, the meatballs, potatoes, and the sweet soup for desert tasted good. She ate well.

Anna could smell the new wood of the cot, as she snuggled down under her own familiar quilt Mother had unpacked. For a few minutes she watched the flicker of light from the stove playing over the log walls, but soon her eyes closed and she was fast asleep.

Chapter Two

When Anna woke up, the morning sun was sending beams in from the little windows. Mother was busy by the table, pouring milk into a tall shiny container.

"Well! You've got your eyes open finally. Look what I've got here. Milk from our own black cow, Mustikki, as your father already named her. Get up and have some with your porridge." Mother's round face crinkled into little lines when she smiled. "It's a beautiful day. Don't sleep it away."

Anna sat up and looked around.

"Where is Liisa?"

"Funny thing. Liisa's already gone to work and I'm glad. I don't know what to do with that girl. Korpis asked your father last evening if she could go and look after their baby today because Korpi-tati is not feeling well. Liisa was quite happy to go. I think she has some idea that she will save up money to go back. Poor girl, she'll be an old lady before she'll get enough money that way."

"Where is Father?"

"He's gone to work on our new house up on the hill. He said he'd be there until noon, when he has to work some more on the field below so that he can plant it—food for Mustikki next win-ter. You can take him some coffee when you have finished your porridge."

Anna stepped into the morning sunshine, when her breakfast was finished. Father said this yard, which was many times bigger than their old yard in Finland, and the woods all belonged to their family—no matter where she went no one would tell her to go away, as often happened in her old home. But then, none of her playmates were here, and she suddenly felt sad. The sad-ness did not last long as Anna looked about at the faintly green-ing world and tried to decide which path to take. One went down the hill to the edge of the dense woods in the valley, and the other up the hill to where the log barn and the chicken coop stood and from where she could hear the sound of Father's axe. She decided to go up the hill, but before she got very far Mother called.

"Don't go yet, Anna. I told you I want you to take your father's coffee." Mother handed her a cloth covered pail. "Can you carry that? I put a cup in for you, too."

Anna started up the hill, carefully holding the pail away from her legs. It was heavy so she had to change it from one hand to the other several times.

As she approached the place where her father was working on the logs for the cabin, she suddenly felt shy. When in Finland, Mother had often talked to her about him and had shown her his picture, but now suddenly he seemed almost a stranger. She could see his arms and shoulders moving back and forth as he smoothed a log with his big axe.

Father was a strong, stocky man with broad shoulders and powerful arms. She stopped a little way from him and just looked, until he noticed her.

"Anna!" he straightened his back and smiled, his grey eyes warming to her. She moved closer to him.

"You've come with coffee for me! Now this is really living. When I was alone, no one brought me coffee. I can tell things are going to be different from now on. What a big girl you are now. When I left, you were just so high," he indicated with his hand. "Sit down there on the log and we'll see what your mother has in the pail." He took the pail from her and set it down on a level stump close by. He took out the coffee jar, the cream and the sugar and the two cups. Then he lifted out a package. "Here is some of Korpi-tati's cake. She is a good neighbor."

Anna and her father settled on the log for their picnic. They ate silently for a few minutes. Anna felt happy sitting beside Father in the sunshine.

"Well, what do you say?" Father finally broke the silence, "this is going to be our new yard. I've left a few birch trees standing, just to remind us of the Old Country. There's the barn with a small pasture behind it. If you listen carefully you can hear Mustikki's bell clinking as she eats her new spring grass. Sh . . . there . . . do you hear it?" Anna nodded. Her father continued. "After awhile you can go and talk to her. Over there on the right, near the barn is the chicken coop. We have twenty-five hens in there. On the other side of the barn, I'll build a stable for our horse, when we get one. I'll have to go and work in a pulp camp before we can afford one. Korpi and I have a good arrangement, I give him milk and eggs for the use of the horse, but I can't do that forever. We need our own."

Anna could hear birds chirping in the birch trees. The logs Father had peeled shone in the sunlight and his big axe was propped up against the tree. Other logs were piled up close by. Anna felt warm and happy. She moved a little closer to Father and he put his arm on her shoulders.

"Yes, my girl, I think this will be a good home for us. We will have to work hard. When I get these walls up, there will be a job for you and Liisa. We will need a lot of moss to chink the walls.

We have a long summer ahead of us before you have to go to school."

Anna was startled. "School!" she exclaimed.

"Yes, of course. You went to school at home, didn't you."

Anna nodded, but she didn't see what that had to do with Canada.

"We're not just visiting here. This is your home now and all children go to school. You'll have to learn English. The people here worked together and built a school house last year, and now the government gives money to pay the teacher. You and Liisa will have to go when school starts in the fall.

Anna had heard English spoken on the boat, in England, and on the train and to her it seemed impossible. "How can I learn English. It doesn't have any words."

Father laughed, "That's what some say of Finnish. You'll learn. You'll be surprised how fast."

"But when I first go, nobody will understand me, and I won't understand anybody," Anna complained.

"Oh, you'll understand everyone except the teacher at first. This community is all Finnish. It's like being back in the Old Country. I wish I could go to school, but I'll have to work to make this bush into a farm."

Anna felt a little better—at least the other children will understand her. But still it would be like starting school all over again. She remembered her first painful day at school in Finland when she felt lost, alone and scared.

Now she had three worries. Father going away for the winter, having to go to school, and having to learn English.

Chapter Three

During the rest of the summer, Anna did not have time to brood about going to school, learning English, or about Father going away. She was too busy.

As her father had warned her, gathering moss for chinking the logs was a big job. She and Liisa went back and forth with their gunny sacks between a place in the woods beyond the clearing and the new cabin. For the first few times they made the trip, the job was fun. The woods were cool, and the green-grey moss soft and springy, as they pulled it by the handfuls into a gunny sack. But soon the chore became tedious. Mosquitoes and black flies tormented them. Anna's ears and neck swelled from blackfly chewings, and Liisa's face was spotted by mosquito bites. Mother felt sorry for them and heated the sauna so that they could get some relief from the itching.

"This is a horrid, horrid place," Liisa cried, her voice going all cracked and funny, as she and Anna sat in the semi-darkness of the hot sauna. "Wh . . . wh . . . why didn't we stay in Kotka? Father had a job. It wasn't as if we *had* to leave like some other poor people."

Anna didn't know what to say. She just hugged her knees. She could feel the sweat trickling down her forehead, stinging her eyes.

"That house," Liisa continued, "it's never going to be finished and we'll be living forever, all jammed together in the sauna dressing room, and I'll never see Kotka again." Liisa's voice broke and Anna could see that she was crying.

"Please don't cry. The house will soon be ready. Father's almost got the roof on. When it's finished everything will be much nicer. Father said we'd have our own room," Anna tried to comfort her sister, but she wouldn't be comforted.

"I don't care, it's still in the bush. There's nobody here. It's a wilderness. I hate it! I hate it! *I hate it!* And it's not fair that Father won't let me go to work in town," she raged.

Anna knew there was nothing she could say to Liisa that would make her feel better, so she just sat with her eyes closed tightly, trying not to hear her voice. She tried to concentrate on how good the heat felt on her ears and neck. She didn't want to think of her sister leaving.

Liisa was quiet when they emerged from the sauna. She had drained her anger for the present.

The moss gathering went on for many days, the filling of the gunny sacks by handfuls, carrying it to the log house, dumping it, and going back and forth, over and over again. Finally Father said they had enough, and they were freed from that daily chore.

Mother and Father chinked the walls. The house was beginning to look almost finished from the outside. Anna thought it would be finished very soon. But Father said, "There's still lots to do. And anyway, now I must go and help Maki with his barn. He doesn't have anyone to help him at all. His children are too little."

Anna was disappointed. Sometimes she just didn't understand grown-ups. Why couldn't he go and help after the house was finished. But she didn't have time to brood because Mother had another project for her.

"We need some sweet soup materials for our winter desserts," Mother said one morning. "Your father says there are lots of blueberries ripening on the far side of our lot, that is, if the bear hasn't got there before us. But first, I want you and Liisa to pick the raspberries along the laneway."

The raspberries grew in brambly patches and sometimes Anna had difficulty reaching the berries. But they were lovely, red and delicious. In the evening, Mother boiled them and put them into jars which Father had bought from town. Their one room became very hot and uncomfortable. One night the heat drove Father to sleep outside. The following morning Father said, "Once we get our house built, we'll use this place as our summer kitchen. We won't bother to move this old cookstove into the house. Maybe I can make some cordwood to sell and buy us a new stove, maybe even a second-hand one."

"That would be good," Mother said, "but there are so many other things we need much more—like a horse, for instance."

"I know, I know. We'll get our horse next spring, after my time at a pulp camp, but in the meantime it won't hurt to cut a bit of cordwood. I'm sure Korpi will be able to lend me his horse for a few days. I'll just have to get up earlier."

As Anna listened to her parents, she was again reminded of her worries, especially of Father being away for the winter.

"Here, Anna, help me carry these jars into the root cellar," Mother called. "Anna, Anna? Do you hear me? Where are you anyway—in such deep thought?"

Anna roused herself and stood up. She stared at the row of jewel-red jars.

"Won't it be nice to open one of these next winter, when the snow is deep and the wind is howling outside?" Mother said.

The root cellar was dark and cool. Father had dug it into the hillside the first summer he arrived. It wasn't just a hole in the hill. He had built a passage way lined in wood, divided by doors into two sections before the cellar proper. The cellar itself had an earthen floor but the ceiling and walls were covered by small round logs. On one side, there was a bin for potatoes, and on the other side, shelves, and below them, smaller bins for beets, carrots, and turnips. Mother kept milk containers on the floor in front of the bins.

Anna could smell the dampish earth and last winter's potatoes in the bin. She liked the smell; it made her think of all the growing things inside the earth.

Mother arranged the jars of raspberries on the upper shelf. "There, now we just have to fill the rest of the shelves and we'll be well off for the winter," she said.

Chapter Four

The next morning Anna and her mother (Liisa had a baby-sitting job again) left with a couple of lard pails and a tin cup for Anna. Mother went ahead on a barely discernible path. The pails clattered in her hand, and the branches swung as she pushed through thickets. She helped Anna balance on a couple of logs that had been thrown over a wet spot. They were finally at the edge of the blueberry area—a level place, but rough and hummocky with fallen logs here and there.

"Keep within calling distance. I don't want you getting lost," Mother warned her, as she settled into a rich patch of blue. "You'll have to be close enough to empty your cup into the pail."

Anna saw another patch just a little distance away, and she began to pick, the first few berries tinkling into her cup. She filled two cupfuls from that patch. Mother had already moved to another place a little farther away. Anna, too, moved to another, a better patch. Anna could feel the warm sun on her head and back. But the clusters of berries still felt cool as she popped a few into her mouth. She emptied her cup into the pail a few more times. She could see Mother bending over in the distance. Then she saw a patch of blue around a large pine tree and she stopped to pick them. She emptied her cup again, before going back to explore farther behind the tree.

"A half hour more should fill our pails and then we can go home," Mother called to her.

Anna picked a couple more cupfuls. She was beginning to get thirsty and tired. She sat on a log for awhile, and listened to the wood sounds, and looked at the pattern of sunlight and shadow on the plants growing on the forest floor.

"Come, girl, get busy. You can't give up yet. The sooner you fill your cup, the sooner we can go home," Mother reminded her.

Anna got up and began to wander about looking for a real good patch. She tried one, but wasn't satisfied; the berries seemed so small. She moved to the next one, and the next until she found a berry patch that was full of berries, bigger than she had seen so far. She ate handfuls of them before starting to fill her cup. She could feel the sweet juice filling her mouth. Finally her cup was filled, and she began to look for Mother. She walked in the direction she thought she had left her. She saw a clump of trees and a fallen log that seemed familiar, but when she got there it looked altogether different. Anna was puzzled. She began to call, "Aiti, Aiti, where are you, where are you?"

But when she listened, she could hear only the wind in the tops of the trees, the chirping of a bird, and the snapping of a branch. She looked around, the trees, the fallen trees, the hummocks all looked the same. She was beginning to feel panicky.

"Aiti, Aiti," she called over and over. But again when she listened she could hear only the wind in the trees. Then she decided she hadn't come far enough; she looked ahead where she thought she recognized the place where she had last seen Mother. *That must be it*, she said to herself. As she scrambled over the hummocks, she was sure she heard twigs breaking and someone talking. But when she stopped to listen, she heard nothing. She called again just in case Mother was close by, "Aiti, Aiti," but there was no answer.

She looked at the berries in her cup. The cup wasn't as full as it had been. She must have lost some scrambling over the hummocks. She was getting more and more thirsty. She took a handful of berries and squished them all in her mouth. This helped a little. She kept going in the direction she thought she should be going. Mother must be here somewhere. She called again, "Aiti, Aiti." But again, she could hear only sounds of the woods. The cracking of branches echoed louder, and the whistling in the trees became more scary, and the shadows of the trees darker. She looked around, and she could no longer see any berry patches. *Where was she? Where was Mother?*

"Aiti, Aiti," her voice was becoming hoarse. "Aiti, Aiti, where are you?" A sob rose in her throat and her eyes stung with tears. She began to run, but stumbled headlong into a hummock and her berries scattered, and her cup flew out of her hand. She lay there a moment. A twig poked her ribs, and a prickly plant scratched her face.

Finally she pulled herself to a sitting position. The woods around her looked strange. There were more dark spruce instead of the pine and birch of the berry patch. Then she remembered adults talking about bears. *What if she met a bear?* She shivered. She felt cold all over. *Was she going to die here? Where was Mother? Had she left her here forever?* She tried to pray, "Help me Jesus, help me."

She got up and began to walk again. The ground under her was getting wetter, the hummocks were larger. She was so tired, she could hardly lift her feet. She sat down with her back against a rock, sobbing until she could sob no more. She closed her eyes. Mother must have gone home and left her. She hardly heard the crackling of the branches and the whining of the wind. She didn't even notice the shadows getting darker and darker. She must have dozed off because when she opened her eyes, it was nearly dark. Then she heard the crashing noise. She knew it was the bear coming for her. She tried to struggle to her feet, but fell back against the rock. Then she heard a voice, several voices! At first she thought she was dreaming—bears don't talk—but then she realized it was people talking and calling, calling her name. She tried to raise her voice.

"Aiti, Isa," she called for Mother and Father, but her voice came out only as a squeak. She tried again. This time her voice came louder. She tried again, and she could hear someone saying, "I hear something."

Now she could hear plainly her name being called. "Anna, Anna." She tried to lift her voice with all her strength. The thought that they might go by without seeing her terrified her.

"Here, I am here," she shouted.

"Anna, Anna," came a man's voice that Anna recognized with great joy, as her father's. She forced herself to stand up even though her feet trembled. She tried to wave her arms so that he would see her. Then she could hear him say, "There she is, there she is. Tell the others we've found her."

Then, to Anna, it looked as if he were taking giant steps towards her, and there he was scooping her into his arms. Mother was right behind him, and she hung on tightly to Anna and Father.

"Where on earth did you get to?" Mother was in tears. "When our pails were full, I began to look for you, but you were nowhere around. I called and called. I walked around where I thought you might be, but I was afraid I'd get lost, so I went home for help. I couldn't understand how you could disappear so fast."

"I was looking for you," Anna whispered into her father's shoulder.

"It's easy to get turned around in the woods," Father said. "You must have started off into the opposite direction from your mother. Anyway you're safe now, and that's what matters."

The other searchers joined them. Anna saw the Makis and Korpis. She wondered what they were all doing there.

Father carried her, and the others followed in single file. When they got to the edge of the clearing behind the barnyard, Anna could hear Liisa's voice. "Anna, Anna, my little sister," she burst out crying.

"She's fine. Don't cry Liisa. Your little sister is fine," Mother assured Liisa and then added, "Did you make the coffee and set the table?" Liisa could only nod.

Anna could hear Mother telling the neighbors to enter.

Father laid Anna on her cot, and Mother wiped her face and arms with a wet cloth.

"My, what a mess you are. Your dress is all torn, and legs all scratched. I better put some medicine on those bigger ones," Mother said, as she bathed the scratches, "Liisa pour the coffee and good neighbors, sit down. All I can say is thank you."

"Yes," Father added, "thank you, thank you for coming to help." He shook hands all around.

For Anna that was a strange evening. She lay on her cot, tired and sore, but at the same time the evening somehow felt almost as if it were Christmas. The neighbors sat and talked. Mother warmed up some supper stew for her, and told her she'd get some of Korpi-tati's piirakka after she finished the stew.

Anna had been too weary to even think about hunger, but once she started eating she realized she was very hungry.

After she finished her supper, Anna could no longer keep her eyes open. The last thing she remembered was her mother tugging at her dress and then slipping the night dress over her head.

Chapter Five

Late in the summer, a new family took a homestead just up the road. The Laine family was living temporarily in a cabin about three miles away, but the man and his sixteen-year-old son came every day to clear land, and to start building a sauna. As well as the son, Tauno, they had four younger children, all girls—Aili, Elsa, Helmi, and Lily. Occasionally, they would all come to their land, and then, Anna, Liisa, and Mother would join them for the afternoon. Mother usually took some pulla, and later when she found out that Mrs. Laine's oven in the old wood stove that was in their cabin did not work, she took bread and sometimes a meat loaf or other oven dishes. For their meals, they set up boards on trestles under the trees. Anna loved these meals. Everything tasted so good. Sometimes Mother scolded her for eating so much.

"I took that food for the Laines. You eat at home."

Anna became friends with Helmi who was only a few months younger. They played in the sweet smelling chips from the logs Laine-seta and Tauno were working on; they used a grove of birch for a house and gathered moss for sofas; they ran down to the little creek that flowed below the hill and splashed around in it, soaking the hems of their skirts. Sometimes Helmi came to Anna's and they played farm under the big pine tree. The roots fanning away from the tree were the stalls, the large pine cones cattle, and the small spruce cones, hens. They played with their dolls. Anna had a store-bought one that Father had given her when they first arrived. Helmi's was a rag doll her mother had made for her. They found a perfect housekeeping place on the big hillside rocks, with an upstairs and a downstairs with nice steps, shelves, flat places, and corners. For both Anna and Helmi, it became a splendid house.

It was a great day for both girls when the Laines finally moved. Helmi and her younger sister Lily spent the whole day at Anna's.

"It's better that you stay here and not get in the way of the workmen." Mother said.

Liisa stayed home with them. Mother went over to help Laine-tati with feeding the helpers. The Korpis and Makis were there as well as some men from farther up the road.

Towards evening, Mother came to milk the cow and to fix supper for them. After they had eaten, Mother announced to Anna's delight, that they would all go to Laine's. But before they left Mother did a strange thing. She caught two hens and handed one over to Liisa and tucked the other, squawking and clucking under her arm. Then she explained, "All the neighbors are bringing hens. That will give the Laines a start on a chicken yard."

Sure enough, when they got to Laines, there was a small makeshift chicken coop that one of the men had hammered together that day, and a chicken fence that was strung around some small trees to make a yard for them.

Laine-tati kept saying over and over again, "You are such good people. Now we will have eggs without having to buy them."

"No, not good people, just pioneers who have to help each other just to survive," one of the men, who Anna did not know, said.

Anna liked the hustle and bustle of so many people around. The evening was warm and comfortable. She and Helmi wandered in and out. The women were setting up mattresses in the loft of the sauna dressing room. Anna thought that was a wonderful place to sleep. A ladder was propped up against the sauna wall to the opening in the ceiling. After the women finished fixing the beds, Helmi and Anna climbed up and tried all the mattresses. They giggled in the darkness. But soon they got tired of lying there, and besides, too much was going on downstairs and outside. As they came down the ladder they found the mothers sitting around the table. Korpi-tati was feeding her baby.

"There you are," Mother said. "Pretty soon we will have to go home. Go and find Liisa and your father."

Helmi and Anna went out.

"Close the door quickly. The moths are just waiting to come into the light," Helmi's mother called after them.

"I can't see," Helmi cried, as she tried to find the lower step. She almost stumbled and grabbed Anna's arm.

"I can't either. Let's just sit here on the steps," Anna suggested.

Gradually their eyes became used to the darkness, and they could see silhouettes of the men at the trestle table. It all seemed so mysterious and exciting, with pipes and cigarettes glowing, and first one voice, then another coming from the dark forms around the table.

Besides the men at the table, they could see another group of dark figures sitting on a big rock just past the hen coop. Anna could hear Liisa's voice and those of the other girls. They were talking to each other, but once in awhile they answered other voices calling to them from the darkness of the trees.

"That's my brother," Helmi said, "He's teasing the older girls. He always does that."

"My sister Liisa has a temper. She'll know how to answer back," Anna assured her friend.

All too soon the evening was over and it was time to leave. Anna walked home companionably by starlight with Mother, Father and Liisa. Even Liisa was in good humour.

Chapter Six

The first day of school was as bad as Anna expected it to be. It started out well enough. Helmi and her sisters, Aili and Elsa, called on her and they walked together along the forest road to the school house. Liisa had absolutely refused to go, and Mother and Father had given in. The weather was warm. Some of the poplar trees were just beginning to turn yellow and the scrub maple splashed crimson over the hills. It was pleasant walking along with Helmi and her sisters. But as soon as they arrived at the school, things changed. Two big boys were standing at the school gate, boys Anna had not seen before. They started talking loudly in Finnish.

"Old Country dumb-bells. We'll have to see what we can do about them."

Aili whispered, "Don't pay any attention. Pretend you don't hear them."

But that didn't work. One of them stuck his foot out, and both Helmi and Anna stumbled into a muddy puddle just beyond the gate. Their hands muddied, their dresses spotted, they both began to cry. After helping Helmi and Anna up and trying to brush off some of the mud, Aili and Elsa both turned on the astonished boys and began to pound them with their fists. Just then the teacher opened the school door and stood for a moment on the steps before she rushed down and walked into the fray, talking loudly in English.

"What is going on here?" She took hold of one of the boys' ears and Elsa by her braid. "Ladies and gentlemen don't act like this. Aarne and Olavi, shame on you for fighting with girls." Then she turned to Aili and Elsa. "You must be new. I don't know you but you'll have to learn that fighting is not allowed."

Aili and Elsa stood straight with their fists pressed to their sides and stared silently at the teacher. By this time Helmi and Anna had stopped crying, but were too afraid to even look at the teacher.

The teacher pointed at the school door; Anna and the others understood they were to go in. She also called the boys. "Aarne and Olavi, I want you in the school room too."

When they got inside, the teacher poured water into a basin from the water pail and the kettle on the heater, and motioned for Helmi and Anna to wash. Then she sat them all down and talked to them very seriously. The girls couldn't understand a word, but they all knew they were being scolded.

Anna sat beside Helmi at a middle-sized desk. She felt thoroughly miserable and in a vague way ashamed before this woman in a white frilly blouse and dark skirt. Anna watched sounds come clacking out of her mouth and she thought, *I'll never, never learn to speak English!* And she thought how lucky Liisa was not to have to go to school.

The rest of the day wore away slowly. After the teacher had taken down their names, Anna and Helmi were given slates and set to copying letters the teacher put on the blackboard. That was easy. Both she and Helmi had already learned their letters in Finland which were the same except for the 'a' with dots and 'o' with dots that made a difference in the pronunciation of the letters. Then they were given sums to do which were even easier. They had done those long ago in Finland.

The teacher smiled at them and patted them on the shoulder. Anna felt a little better. She looked around the school room when she finished the sums. She could hear the rustle of paper, the scratch of pens, and the occasional shuffling of feet. The double desks were arranged in rows with the big ones on the right of the room facing the front, the middle sized desks made the middle row and the small ones were on the left. The teacher's desk was on a raised platform in front. Behind her on the wall hung the clock and the picture of the King and Queen. Anna was fascinated by this picture. The Queen had such a long neck, and it was completely covered in pearls; the King's chest was full of ribbons, and she was surprised to see that he looked a lot like the picture of the Tsar she had seen at home.

At recess the four girls stuck together. They sat at Elsa's and Aili's desk. The other children went outside. The teacher looked at them a couple of times as if to speak, but then gave up.

After recess the teacher gave them each a Primer from the blue-grey chest beside her desk, and had one of the other girls explain that they were to bring three cents for the book.

Anna could hear Aili mutter aloud to Elsa, "A child's book."

The teacher said, "I beg your pardon?"

Aili blushed, but kept her eye on the teacher.

The teacher finally turned around and began to busy herself with some of the other classes.

Anna looked at the Primer. There was some writing in the first part of the book, with pictures of a hen, a dog, a cat, and a pig. Anna couldn't quite figure out what was going on in the story. It looked as if the hen was doing something. There were other fascinating pictures of animals and people, but when could she ever learn to read those funny words.

When lunch time came, the teacher asked one of the older girls named Aino to explain to them in Finnish that they were to go outside. Anna was surprised how talkative everyone was. They all spoke Finnish once they were out of the school room. Aino and the other girls told Aili and Elsa how pleased they were that they had taken on Aarne and Olavi. "They think they're some kind of lords. Everyone is going to laugh at them now."

In the afternoon the teacher called Anna, Helmi, and her sisters to the blackboard. They were uncomfortable at first, especially Elsa and Aili, who blushed and shuffled from one foot to the other. They whispered the sounds as the teacher started on the phonetics of the alphabet and on a few simple words.

Anna was nervous too, but she was also fascinated when the teacher sounded out the first few words—C A T, H A T, D O G.

After she had written the words in her notebook as the teacher requested, she tried to sound out some of the words in her Primer but her tongue became hopelessly tangled in the funny letter combinations. After her first bit of encouragement she was again dashed down. The letters just did not sound out anything sensible.

Chapter Seven

In the shortening autumn days, school settled into a routine. Gradually, very gradually, Anna began to understand words here and there. She became less frustrated after she discovered that all the words could not be sounded, and that some of them just had to be memorized. And whizzing ahead in arithmetic made her feel good. Also, the teacher did not seem to be such a frightening person anymore.

There were miserable days too, when Elsa and Aili skipped school, or when Aarne and Olavi decided that she needed some shaking up, but those days passed into more pleasant ones.

One brilliant Saturday she helped Father, Mother, and Liisa dig up the potatoes. The sky was as blue as it could be and the far hills were a smoky indigo. The earth smelled pungent and squished under her shoe. Her job was to pick up the smaller potatoes as Father opened up the hill and chose the larger ones into his pail. Mother and Liisa worked together in another row.

"Come, what's happening to my helper," Father said, as Anna began to slow down. Her back was sore and her arms were tired, but mostly she was bored with the job.

"Come on, hurry. You're going to be left behind if you dawdle. Why don't you count the potatoes and see how many you can fit into the pail."

Father tried to encourage her in various ways. He asked riddles, he told stories from Finland, and even asked her to teach him some English words.

Mother brought them coffee and sweet bread half way through the morning, and again in the afternoon. For dinner they went home for the meat-and-potatoes stew that Mother had prepared early that morning, and left at the back of the stove to simmer. That was a welcome break from the field. But even with all these diversions, Anna was bone weary by the time they got to the end of the last row. She nodded off in the middle of supper. Mother laid Anna on her cot until it was time for the sauna.

The next morning, when Anna woke up she wondered why the room looked suddenly so light-filled. When she looked out of the window everything was covered in snow; the trees were heavy with it and the smallest twigs were thickly coated.

"Winter comes early in this country," Mother remarked as Anna was looking out of the window.

"Haven't I told you that this country is no good," Liisa lashed out at them suddenly. "Now Father won't be able to finish the house and we'll all be stuck in this place all winter. We'll go crazy."

"Please, Liisa, don't start that again. Be reasonable," Mother looked at her and shook her head.

"I'm the one who is reasonable. We had a perfectly good home in Kotka. Kotka by the sea where winter does not come in October." Liisa was trying to gulp down her tears.

"What time are you supposed to go to Korpi's?" Mother changed the subject.

"At noon," Liisa mumbled.

Anna couldn't understand why Liisa was angry about the snow. She could hardly wait to go outside. The snow made everything brighter. But then Liisa was angry about everything most days.

Anna dressed in a hurry, had breakfast and raced outside. The snow was just made for snowballs and snowmen. She made a big snowman and built a snowball fence around her pretend barn. She found Father's skis and made tracks in the field. When she came in for lunch, Mother scolded her for being so wet, but she had had a glorious morning.

To Anna's disappointment it rained the next day, melting her snowman into a bedraggled looking lump. In another week, the snow was gone except for a few patches in the deep woods.

Father went back to work on the new house.

"If the weather holds long enough for me to get in the windows and doors," Father said the following morning as he was getting dressed to go outside, "then I could work inside even if it gets colder, maybe, just maybe I could get it finished. It would be nice for you and the girls to be moved in by the time I go to the bush camp. But it all depends on the weather, and maybe it's unreasonable to expect good weather any more."

It was later that morning that the surprise came. Men began arriving, carrying saws and hammers. Korpi-seta and Maki-seta both left a parcel with Mother. "My wife sent some lunch and she said she would be here at noon to help," Korpi-seta explained.

"What's going on?" Mother called, as the men were heading up the path towards the new house.

"Oh, just a bit of neighborly help," Maki-seta laughed. "There'll be more in a little while."

Mother turned to Liisa and Anna, her face creased in smiles. "Well my girls, it looks as if we will get into our new house after all. Won't that be wonderful!" She just stood there smiling and smiling. Anna was surprised. She didn't know that Mother wanted the house so badly. She had never said anything about it.

"I just can't stand here," Mother started to open the two parcels on the table, one was wrapped in brown paper and the other in a gunny sack. The gunny sack contained turnips and carrots and in the other there was a hunk of meat.

"That must be moose meat. It's much darker than beef," Mother said.

"Ugh," said Liisa.

"What's the matter with you? It's perfectly good meat," Mother turned to Liisa.

"Yes, for this country it is," Liisa retorted.

"And what did you, a fine lady, eat in Kotka—mostly sausages and fish," Mother was getting upset.

"I'd rather have Finnish sausages any time than that wild meat."

"That's enough," Mother commanded. "Get some dry wood, birch if you can find any. We want a good hot fire to start the meat. Anna, you check the tea kettle. I'll have to make a big pot of coffee for their mid-morning coffee." Mother began to prepare the meat for roasting.

Laine-seta and Tauno, as well as several other men Anna did not know, came within the next hour.

"It's just about time to take the men their mid-morning coffee," Mother said. "Liisa, you cut up some pulla and fix up a couple of pails with cups, spoons, sugar, and cream. Anna, don't go anywhere. You are going to help Liisa take the coffee to the house."

Anna felt that the day had turned into some kind of feast day, as she and Liisa carried the coffee to the men at the building.

The men themselves acted as if it were a holiday. They were talking and laughing over the rhythmic tapping of the hammers and the buzz of the saws.

As the girls neared the building, someone shouted, "Coffee time! Here comes the coffee."

Father took the pail from Anna and lifted out the cups. the sugar and cream. Liisa opened the pail with the pulla and then started pouring the coffee.

"Be sure to give me lots," Tauno called to her. Anna could see Liisa's face redden, but she couldn't figure out if Liisa liked or disliked his comments.

The coffee steamed in the cool air, as the men crowded around to get their cups.

"How is it going, Anna," Helmi's father asked her.

She didn't answer. She didn't know what to say. Grown-ups always asked questions that were hard to answer.

"You and Helmi seem to be doing fine at school," he continued.

Anna just nodded.

"Cat got your tongue?" Father demanded. "It's rude not to answer when someone talks to you."

"Never mind," Helmi's father said. "You will be glad to hear that Helmi is coming later with her mother."

Anna smiled up at him and avoided Father's eyes.

While the men were drinking their coffee, Anna inspected the house. The big kitchen was beginning to look like a real room with windows in, and the floor boards nailed down. The two bedrooms beside the kitchen were already partitioned.

Anna became more and more excited. Liisa and she would have a room, and the sleeping cots wouldn't need to be folded every morning, and they wouldn't be bumping into each other all the time. This was bigger than their place in Kotka. And as Father would say, it was their own.

Anna's excitement lasted all day, and she was eager to do anything Mother asked her to do.

The men had to be fed in two shifts. Anna was set upon her knees on a chair so that she could reach the dish pan and she washed, and washed—cutlery, plates, cups—until her arms ached. Half way through the second batch, Helmi came and the two of them worked together. Anna's excitement was still carrying her along, and she was happy.

The day truly turned out to be a feast day. More women came in the afternoon and brought cakes and sweet buns. She and Helmi helped to take the afternoon coffee to the men and the two of them had a wonderful time eating the goodies. They listened to the women talking as they prepared supper. They played with Korpi-tati's baby.

In the evening when the people had gone and they had had their sauna, Mother and Father were looking at Eaton's catalogue by the lamp-lit table. Anna and Liisa were already in their cots. Anna lay listening to her parents as she watched flickering lights from the stove move along the ceiling and walls.

Father was saying, "Thanks to our neighbors, we could move in tomorrow, but maybe we should paint the floor first. I'll put in the old box stove I got from Korpi so that I can heat the place. By that time the kitchen stove will come. What do you say?"

"The painted floors would be easier to keep clean. Look at this floor, it never looks clean, and I'm certainly not going to do my mother's trick of scrubbing with sand. I can wait for another couple of weeks, especially since I had already given up hope of getting in this fall."

"That's what we will do then," Father said as he continued leafing through the catalogue. "I wish we could order some of this furniture, like a dresser and some chairs but we just can't, that stove will clean us out."

"All that will come in time," Mother said.

Chapter Eight

To the excitement of getting into their new home was added a new excitement at school. Helmi's sisters, Aili and Elsa, had missed a lot of school during the fall, mostly because they hated being lumped in with the little kids in reading and writing. Helmi had told Anna that her sisters were planning to quit school anyway so they didn't care how they did. But when they heard about the Christmas concert, they decided to stay until Christmas. It was rumored that there would be candies and a present for each pupil.

Anna continued her lopsided progress, doing well in arithmetic but struggling with reading, writing, and spelling. She could read the story of the Little Red Hen, the verses about Humpty Dumpty, Jack and Jill, and many of the other rhymes to herself, but when the teacher asked them to stand in front of her desk and made them read aloud, she was in trouble. One day when she had to read aloud from the story of Goldilocks and the Three Bears, her tongue got all tangled up in the words. It started with the very first words—the three bears. She couldn't pronounce the two words starting with "th." She said "da tree." The teacher stopped her.

"The, the, put your tongue between your teeth, like this." She tried to show Anna what she meant.

Anna could hear some giggles behind her, but when she pronounced "bears" as "beers" everyone started laughing aloud.

Anna could feel her face getting hot, and she had to stiffen her face so that she wouldn't cry.

The teacher too, smiled and turned to the blackboard, and wrote "ea" and the words near, fear, tear, underlining the "ea."

"All right, let's settle down. That's a perfectly natural mistake to make. We just looked at these words yesterday in our spelling and quite often "ea" makes the "ee" sound. Never mind Anna, it is very confusing, and these people laughing have made the same mistakes."

But the teacher's words did not comfort her much. Anna knew that she would be teased mercilessly once school was out. She would be called "Old Country dumb-bell" over and over again. And she was right. Olavi and Aarne started at her the minute recess started.

"Da tree beers."

"Da tree beers."

"What does the Old Country dumb-bell say—da tree beers—that's what." Finally Aili threatened them and told them to stop. They were just a little scared of her.

However, all that was soon forgotten when the Christmas concert preparations began. There were Christmas songs for the whole school to learn; good readers were given recitations; parts were given out for the various skits and dialogues.

Anna was pleased that she was picked with the other middle-sized girls for a drill routine. They marched around the stage, made turns, and moved their wooden batons in time to music. Anna was glad she didn't have anything to say. In the afternoon, she could hardly wait to get home. Father had painted the floors of the new house a bright, orangy yellow. Mother had hung embroidered curtains made from flour sacks. When the floors dried, she put down the woven rag mats she had brought from Finland. To Anna it all looked so pretty. But the greatest excitement came when the kitchen stove arrived, and they began to move in. Father went to get it from town with Korpi's horse and sleigh, and Laine-seta came over to help Father carry it into the house.

Anna was fascinated by all the carved decorations on it—flowers, leaves, and strange creatures around the firebox and the oven door. Later that same day, they carried the tables and benches and other household goods from the sauna dressing room up to the house. Father had made a kitchen cupboard and another table and some shelves from rough boards he had on hand. Liisa and Mother were able to put away the dishes, pots, and groceries. Even the big steamer trunk was carried in from the shed by the barn and put into Mother's and Father's bedroom. Liisa found a wooden crate for their bedroom, which she covered with blue and red material that Korpi-tati had given her. Father set up their cots and Mother gave them one of the mats she had.

The new kitchen stove worked beautifully. Mother made an extra special meal with blueberry pie for dessert. Everyone, even Liisa, was in good spirits.

"It will be easier for me to leave for the bush camp with the three of you in this snug little house," Father remarked as they were eating.

"You're not going before Christmas, are you?" Mother looked startled.

"I don't know for sure. It depends on what is available and what contractors are hiring. If I can get in with a reliable company with good timber limits, I'll have to go even if it is before Christmas," Father explained.

Mother just nodded and looked sad. After awhile she said, "I guess the girls and I will be all right and we have neighbors, not like Mrs. Lehtonen with her children. They tell me she was the only person here during the first winter. Mr. Lehtonen was working in town and only came out on Saturday nights and went back on Sunday. I would have found that too much."

Father suddenly put his hands to his forehead. "That reminds me. Voi, voi—I knew there was something else I had to do. I have to finish your skis! You will need them when we get lots of snow. I started them last spring but did not quite finish. I still have to put in the toe straps and of course, oil them. I'll do that tomorrow. It won't take me long."

Chapter Nine

Winter came in earnest a few days after they settled into the new house. First came a huge snow storm. The snow was coming down in large pretty flakes on Saturday night when Mother, Liisa, and Anna came in from the sauna. When they woke up on Sunday morning the whole world was covered in snow, not decoratively as in the first October snowfall, but with the full force of a northern winter. The branches of trees and shrubs were weighed down and the chicken coop was almost out of sight. When Father opened the kitchen door, snow that had been piled up against it fell into the kitchen.

"I can see that we need a porch," Father said, as he started to sweep the snow out and off the step.

Anna could hardly wait to get outside.

She helped Father tramp a path to the barn and the chicken coop. Father had to shovel the snow from the barn door before they could get in.

"We'll feed and water the cow so that your mother can come to milk her."

The barn was warm with the smell of Mustikki, the cow. Anna could hardly see her at first because of the darkness. The two small windows were frosted over and half covered with snow. When her eyes got used to the dimness she could see Mustikki lifting her head and looking at them. She mooed a couple of times as if to say, "where have you been?"

"She's hungry. She wants her hay and water," Father said. He went to the big wooden barrel in the corner, took a bucket from a nail on the wall and dipped it into the barrel and placed the water in front of the cow.

Anna watched Mustikki bury her face and draw up the water in great gulps.

"Thirsty, wasn't she," Father said as he lifted the pail away. Then he took a pitchfork to the haystack near the barn door and pulled out a chunk of hay and carried it into the barn and laid it in the manger in front of Mustikki. The hay rustled and sent a summery fragrance into the warmth of the barn.

Then they went to the chicken coop. Father scooped some wheat out of the sack, that was set into a box beside the door, and scattered it among the chickens. They rushed from all corners of the coop to get at the grain, their great clucking quieted as they ate.

"Their water is low," Father said. "Will you go into the barn and bring back some water with that little pail? "I'll fix up a bit of a fire."

With their chores done they headed towards the house.

"There's a wind coming up." Father pointed to the trees in the northwest. "When all this snow is blown into hard drifts it will be difficult to get around."

Father was right about the wind. It came up suddenly, and soon their house seemed to be in the middle of a snowy whirlwind. Anna watched out of the window. Mother wouldn't let her go outside. "You'll freeze to death," she said.

The new kitchen stove burned brightly and the box stove beside it added to the warmth. Mother and Father read newspapers and magazines that had come in the mail from Finland. Liisa studied the Eaton's catalogue, and Anna tried to make sense of the stories and poems from a book she had brought home from the school library. They had their morning and afternoon coffee companionably at the kitchen table.

"Look Anna," Father pointed out of the kitchen window. The air was momentarily clear as the wind slackened. "Look out there—look, you can see the world." Father's eyes twinkled the way they did when he teased her.

Mother stood up behind Father to see what he was pointing at. "What are you talking about? What world?"

"See that blueness between the hills. That's the Westfort mountain. It looks on the ships on Lake Superior and on the trains that go east and west and finally connect with ships that go all over the world. It's our link to the world."

"What an imagination you have!" Mother laughed as she rubbed Father's neck and shoulders.

"But that's true, isn't it?" Father demanded.

"Yes, and that's the road right into town and then straight to Finland," Liisa broke into the conversation. "In March, I will be sixteen. I'm going to work to earn enough money to get a ticket back to Finland."

Mother and Father were surprised by Liisa's sudden outburst and somehow for Anna the nice feeling of the moment was broken.

Father just said quietly: "Yes, I did say you could go to work."

Mother busied herself with the stove, putting in wood, and moving the kettle and pots about.

"Since we are on the topic of going," Father steered the talk away from Liisa's outburst. "I think as soon as this storm is over and I can get out, I'll ask Korpi for his horse and go into town. I'll bring home feed for the cow and chickens, and any groceries you will need. At the same time, I can scout around the bush company offices to find out about jobs."

"It's only a month to Christmas. Can't you go right after Christmas?" Mother begged.

"As I told you before, that depends on the kinds of jobs that are available. I'd like to get a good contractor. With some you don't get decent food, a sauna, or decent camps, and some of their forest limits are poor. If I can get a good one, I'll have to go. I have to make enough money to buy a horse and gear—both wagon and sleigh. With a horse, I could do so much more. We have some wood on this land. I could make a load of cordwood and get some cash when we need it. Laine told me that he's heard that they're starting to work on some of the township roads next spring. I could get more money if I could get work with a horse."

All this talk about going made Anna sadder and sadder. If Father went before Christmas he wouldn't be here for the concert.

The wind started up again and the snow whirled around the house.

Chapter Ten

By the following morning, the fierce wind had stopped. but it was still very cold. Mother wasn't going to let Anna go to school, but when Helmi came to the door she relented. Mother made her wear two pairs of stockings, one the heavy brown pair she hated, two sweaters under her coat, and she wrapped a big wool scarf over her head and face so that just her eyes were showing.

"The snow drifts are so big. I hate see them go," Mother commented as she watched Anna and Helmi out of the window.

"That snow is so hard that they'll be able to walk over it and the bush road is sheltered, and anyway I think I'll walk a piece after them to see how they're doing," Father said.

Anna and Helmi skipped and hopped along the tops of the snow banks. The snow had been packed so hard that it felt almost like a sidewalk. In other places the snow had been whirled and twirled into frozen waves. They raced up one wave and down another. They fell, they scrambled, and they giggled. They were having so much fun that they didn't even see Father as he watched them from the top of the last hill before the school house.

The teacher opened the door for them as they climbed the school steps.

"You poor children. Look at all that frost around your scarves and hats, and even your eyelashes," the teacher exclaimed.

She unwound their scarves and helped with the coats.

"I guess you haven't suffered. You are so warmly dressed. Leave your sweaters on. It's still chilly in here."

As Anna looked around the school room she was surprised that only a couple of girls, Aino and Saimi, who lived close by, were sitting at a desk that had been moved close to the stove. No one else was there.

"Come, we'll move your desk close to the stove, too. I don't suppose anyone else is coming. We'll just have a bit of an open-ing, and then we'll work on things that you have the most trou-ble with. Anna and Helmi, I think that means that you will spend most of the day reading. I would like your reading to catch up with your arithmetic. I think after Christmas you should be able to leave the Primer and start on the First Book. Aino and Saimi, maybe you should work on your parts in the Christmas play. Your parts are the longest and we don't want to do any new work and leave Olavi and Reino behind.

Anna enjoyed the day. She didn't even mind reading for the teacher when the whole school wasn't listening. Even mistakes in pronunciation that were so upsetting ordinarily, just made her giggle.

The teacher was much more friendly. She laughed and talked with them as if they weren't in school at all. At noon she made hot chocolate and shared cookies with them. By the afternoon, the schoolroom warmed up and they were able to move their desks back to the proper places.

The teacher gave Anna and Helmi a spelling lesson and a writ-ing lesson but the rest of the time they continued reading the Primer. The promise of a new book made them read on and on— the story of *Henny Penny*, *The Ginger Bread Boy*, *The Town Musicians*. When four o'clock came there were only a few pages left.

"Well, girls. It looks as if you will have no problem getting through the Primer by Christmas. You both have done very well. In such a short time you have learned a lot."

Anna felt warm from this praise, as well as warm from the heat of the big stove. When it was time to go, the teacher wound the scarves around their heads and made sure their wrists were covered by their sleeves and their mitts.

Chapter Eleven

Christmas was only two weeks away. More and more time at school was taken by the Christmas concert practices. The drill routine with batons was going well. It was fun marching and doing the baton movements to the music coming from the teacher's gramophone. Anna and Helmi walked home in the afternoons laughing and chattering. Sometimes they played games with the long shadows of trees the mid-winter sun cast over the road. They jumped over the shadows, pretending they were jumping over the trees. One afternoon, they watched the moon as it seemed to be following them. They decided to try each going in opposite directions to see which one the moon would follow. They got into a friendly argument when both claimed the moon's following.

It was after one of these happy afternoons that Anna was shocked to see her father's packsack in the middle of the kitchen floor all ready to go. Father and Mother were both at the table having coffee and Father was dressed in his heavy plaid shirt and his mackinaw pants. Anna knew then that he was leaving for a pulpwood camp. She could feel a large lump forming in her throat and she had to blink hard to keep tears from spilling over. She stared at her father. She couldn't say anything.

"Come, my girl, don't just stand there, come and have some coffee. Your mother just took the pulla out of the oven."

"Why do you have to go before Christmas? Are you coming home for Christmas?" she finally blurted out.

"I have to go now because I have to make some money for us. No, I can't come home for Christmas because it's too far away. I don't like being away for Christmas either, not one bit, but the way things are I have to go. I hope that I won't have to be away for another Christmas. But now we need a horse. Wouldn't it be great to have our own horse, to go for a ride anytime we wanted to? Come, smile Anna. The time will go fast," Father tried to cheer her up.

Mother placed a coffee cup with a generous amount of milk before Anna and gave her a slice of pulla.

Anna took a sip of coffee and nibbled on the pulla but she did not feel like smiling. *Now Father would not be at the concert and see her in the drill. And anyway, how could they get along without him?* As if the answer to these inside-the-head questions, Father began to explain about the wood.

"The first pile is drier and I've split some kindling that will last a little while. I'm sure I have enough wood sawed to last you."

"We'll get along. I have cut and sawn wood, I know how. Don't worry about us. Liisa, Anna, and I will survive." Mother sounded sure of herself, and that made Anna feel better.

"I must be off." Father stood up. "I have to meet the other men at Moving Post corner. Maki's son is taking us into town with his horse and we catch the train at midnight for the pulpwood camps."

Father touched Anna on the shoulder.

"You be a good girl with Mother. Help her as much as you can."

Mother followed him outside. When she came in Anna could see she was very sad. Instead of sitting down again, Mother began to clear the table. "Come help me, Anna. You can wash these dishes. I'll have to fill the lamps before it gets altogether dark, and before I go to feed and milk the cow. I'll have to clean the lamp chimneys, and I might as well do the lantern too. Your sister won't be home until later from Korpi's."

It seemed to Anna that Mother was making a big fuss about chores that were done every night.

Later the three of them sat around the table. Anna did her homework, Liisa embroidered on a table cloth and Mother knitted on Father's gray wool sock. No one felt like talking. Anna could hear the fire crackling in the stove and clock ticking in the corner.

"Are you almost finished?" Mother asked Anna after awhile. "Do you want some cocoa? I think I'll make myself a cup before we go to sleep. How about you Liisa?"

Later when they were getting ready for bed, Mother came into their room with an armful of blankets. "Here are some extra covers for you. It will get cold tonight. I'm nervous about the fire, so I don't want to leave too big a fire. It will probably go out, unless I happen to wake up to stoke it"

When Anna lay in her cot that night, everything seemed so different. She felt as if there were a big, black hole somewhere in the house.

Chapter Twelve

They gradually began to get used to Father's absence. There were more chores for Anna and Liisa, because Mother had to carry all the water for the cow and chickens, as well as for use in the house. She had to drag the hay from the haystack, and do many other jobs that Father did when he was home.

At school, the atmosphere was getting more and more electric, as the day for the Christmas concert approached. It was exciting for Anna, until the problem of the costume came up. For their drill routine the teacher, with the help of the older girls, had made costumes from pink crepe paper, dresses with flared skirts and short butterfly sleeves. They were very pretty. But the problem came when the teacher asked if Anna could leave off her heavy long-sleeved vest for the concert night. But Mother absolutely forbad it. She wasn't going to have her going undressed in thirty below weather! No amount of tearful pleading could move Mother. The bigger girls who were helping with the costumes made rude remarks about her mother in Anna's hearing. The girls who did the drill with her, whispered among themselves and wouldn't talk to her. Olavi and Aarne started calling her "thick vest." When on stage she could feel all eyes on her. This made her forget her movements. She kept turning in the wrong direction and throwing all the others out. They had to keep going over and over the same movements, and she kept making the same mistakes. It went so badly that the teacher made them stay after four to practice some more. The other girls were really angry by this time.

Anna heard someone say, "She shouldn't be in it. Why doesn't the teacher drop her?" Anna went home that afternoon feeling gray as the mid-winter day itself.

That evening she could hardly eat her supper.

"What's the matter with you?" Mother demanded. "Are you sick?"

Anna just shook her head and wouldn't say anything. She was afraid to because she was so close to tears.

"Cat got your tongue? Maybe I should give you some castor oil," Mother said.

Anna shook her head vigorously, and finally she was able to say, "No, no, I'm not sick. I just feel sad."

She hoped that Mother would think it was because Father was away, and wouldn't question her any more.

The last few practices did go well, and even the problem of the vest sleeves was partly solved. The teacher folded them and pinned them securely under the pink butterfly sleeves of the costume. They felt bulky but at least they weren't showing. And the others soon forgot the problem in the commotion of the last days before the concert. There were many things to do. The big boys got the Christmas tree and set it up; the big girls helped the teacher decorate the tree and tie the candles to the branches. The smaller children were set to making red and green paper chains, which where then strung around the room; Anna's class covered spruce cones with red crepe paper to make pretend holly berries to go with the green boughs.

The school room looked and smelled pretty by the day of the concert. Sheets were hung for stage curtains and everything was set. The teacher sent them home early so that they could all get back in good time for the concert.

After all the chores were done, Mother, Liisa, and Anna got ready to leave for the school house.

"I think we'll walk. I'm not at all sure of the ski trail and that one hill is so steep for night skiing."

The stars and the half moon gave them enough light to find the path in the snow. The snow squeaked under foot, and their scarves frosted from their breath.

As they approached the school house, the candles, already lit on the window sills, flickered a welcome into the darkness. Other figures in the dark were hurrying towards the school. Some had lanterns which bobbed back and forth to the walker's gait. Sleighbells tinkled and harnesses squeaked as horses and sleighs travelled towards the school house.

When the school door opened, Anna could feel the warm spruce-scented air embracing her. The room itself looked different from the way it had looked in the afternoon. The light of the oil lamps and the candles transformed it into a storybook place. The red and green crepe paper chains and the other streamers, the tinsel on the tree, and even the make-believe holly berries glowed in the flickering lights.

"Let's sit over there at a desk. These benches will be too hard on the back," Mother said to Liisa.

Anna saw Helmi peeping from behind the curtain beckoning to her.

The coats of the pupils were piled up on a desk in one corner, and the costumes were laid out on some more desks. The teacher had told them earlier that day, that most of them would have to sit in the first two rows until their time came. But the drill routine came right after the school song and one recitation. Anna's group had to start getting ready right after the school song.

Anna had a moment of panic when the Junior Fourth girl, who was helping her, couldn't find the safety pins for her sleeves. The girl made a rude remark in Finnish about her vest. But the pins were found, and after some scrambling, they stood behind the curtain, ready to go on when the recitation finished. Anna tried to keep her mind on the first series of moves and not on all those people sitting out there in the school room.

There was much clapping when they took their bows, even though Anna couldn't remember a thing about their performance—it was all over so quickly. The others seemed to be happy so Anna decided she must have done everything right. She sat happily in the front row watching the plays and recitations. There were two more school songs for which everyone went on stage—one in the middle of the program and one at the end. The last song was about Santa Claus. Just as their song ended, there was a sound of bells and Santa leaped into the school room from the door behind the stage.

He looked a little strange to Anna—his costume was different from Joulupukki in Finland, but he did speak Finnish. He made them laugh as he told them about his problems crossing the ocean on his sleigh from Lapland, "But then, you don't want to hear about my problems, you want to know what's under the tree and in this pack. Do I have any helpers?" Two men stepped up and began to hand out the the bags of candy from under the tree and the teacher helped Santa with the individuals gifts. Anna waited for her name to be called. Some of the children were already opening their packages—Anna saw lacy handkerchiefs, ties, small celluloid dolls, pretty pins, books, balls, and toys.

When Anna's name was finally called, she received a small oblong package. When she opened it she found a comb in a pink case. She tried not to show her disappointment. She put the parcel into the bag with the fruit and candy.

Mother was talking to Helmi's mother and another woman Anna did not know. Anna stood and waited. Others around the school room were talking in groups. No one seemed to be in a hurry to leave. The men went about blowing out the candles from the tree and the window sills. Only the oil lamps were still lit. It seemed to Anna that the story book look of the school room was fading, and she wished Mother would stop talking so they could leave.

Finally Mother put on her coat and said to Anna, "Do you have everything?" Anna nodded and hurried towards the door before Mother found someone else to talk with.

As they started out along the road, a horse and sleigh pulled up beside them. It belonged to family farther up the road from their place. As well as his family, Helmi, her sisters and her mother were already in the sleigh.

"There's room for more," the man said. "Come, we go right by your place. Come, hop on."

"Kiitos," Mother said. "A ride will be really nice."

The others in the sleigh made room for them and they climbed on to the blanket covering the hay.

Anna sat happily between Mother and Liisa and held tightly to her bag of goodies. The sleigh bells tinkled and the snow squeaked under the runners and the horse's hooves. The sky was full of stars and the dark woods seemed almost friendly. And Anna hardly remembered she had had any other home.

Chapter Thirteen

On Christmas Eve and Christmas day they missed Father even though Mother tried to do all the Christmas things they were used to in Finland.

With money she had saved during their journey over, she had ordered a ham, rice, raisins, almonds, and fresh yeast, through Korpi-seta when he went for groceries. They had enough flour and sugar to last until Father returned. Mother and Liisa made some ginger cookies, and on the morning of Christmas Eve, Mother made a special pulla with cardamom, and glazed with sugar. The house smelled nice. For Anna all would have been perfect if only Father were home.

The sauna had to be heated. Mother gave the task to Liisa. In the afternoon they went to get a tree. They found a pretty, well-formed spruce on the edge of the clearing.

"It's too small," Liisa complained.

"It will have to do. This is the biggest we can handle at the moment," Mother said.

They got it up without too much trouble. Mother found a nice, smooth, short, half-log left over from when the house was built. While Anna and Liisa held on, she bored a hole into it with father's auger.

"That's pretty straight," Mother said as she looked at the tree. "Now, let's get it decorated. Anna, get the small box from my trunk in the bedroom. I brought a few little trinkets from home. There are even a few candles in there. Liisa, you hang a few of those ginger cookies and I think we can find some shiny paper somewhere around."

Anna admired the tree when they finished decorating. She could hardly wait for darkness to come for the candles to be lit.

Mother had put the ham into the oven after she had taken out the pulla. Its smell started mingling with the bread smell. She also prepared a turnip loaf, and a carrot and beet salad. The day before, Anna had skied with her mother to the root cellar and helped her bring some potatoes and turnips and a jar of raspberries and blueberries.

Mother started the rice pudding before milking and the other outside chores, and asked Anna to stir it while she was in the barn.

"Liisa, you set the table. Get the linen cloth from the trunk. What will we do for candle holder? Never mind. I'll think of something," Mother said as she went out of the door with her milk pail.

"You did a nice job of heating the sauna, Liisa. It's just right, nice and hot, but not burning hot," Mother said as the three of them sat on the top bench in its shadowy darkness. The small lamp on the dressing room side behind the little window was its only light.

The white cloth on the table, the lit candles on the Christmas tree, the red mitts Mother had knit for both her and Liisa helped Anna feel that it was really Christmas. Liisa had embroidered a pair of pillow-cases for Mother, and a pretty collar for Anna with Korpi-tati's help, and Anna had made fancy pincushions at school for both Liisa and Mother. The reading of the Christmas gospel and the singing of 'Enkeli Taivaan' added to the festivity.

Mother had even remembered to put an almond into the rice. Liisa found it and seemed pleased and blushed. Custom said that the person finding it would get married soon. But under all this cheer lurked loneliness and sadness because Father was not with them. A couple of times Anna could see that Mother was close to tears, as she fingered the pillowcases and patted the pincushion.

Christmas Day was even lonelier. They ate what was left over from Christmas Eve. Mother read the Finnish magazines she had received from her mother the week before. Liisa read a little but mostly she examined Eaton's catalogue. Anna read a book about a pioneer girl she had brought from school. And, of course, the necessary chores had to be done.

On Boxing Day, they walked over to the school for a church service. Anna watched and listened to the pastor in his black coat and his white-winged collar. When she closed her eyes when he chanted the liturgy she could almost imagine herself back in Finland. With her eyes open this was impossible. The bare little school was not at all like the beautiful church in Kotka. But the story from the gospel was the same, and she felt warm and happy.

On New Year's Eve, they invited Helmi's family to their house. They all came. Helmi's father and brother were going to a pulpwood camp after New Year's, so they were still at home.

The grown-ups drank coffee and ate, and talked about the Old Country. Liisa, Elsa, Aili, and Matti just sat and listened. Helmi and Anna played for awhile with their dolls in the bedroom with Lily joining them when she felt like it, but when Helmi's father started asking riddles they forgot about the dolls and joined the others in the kitchen. Helmi's father seemed to have an unending supply of riddles and all kinds of rhymes and poems. As well, he knew many songs and with all the repetitions and choruses soon everybody was singing.

But then suddenly he stopped and said: "This is New Year's Eve and we've got important things to do. Eeva," he addressed Anna's mother. "Do you have any tin? I brought some but I don't know if it is enough."

The older girls looked expectantly at him. They knew what he was about to do. He was going to tell their fortunes.

"Who's first?" Laine-seta asked, when he was ready with the tin. "What about you Lily?" He said. "We'll start with the youngest." Lily just smiled and nodded her head vigorously.

The tin was heated to liquid form and then poured into cold water. The shape that it twisted itself into was then read.

They had great fun trying to decide what the funny shapes meant. There was much teasing when both Liisa and Tauno got what looked like rings. Anna got what looked like a boat and Laine-seta wanted to know where she was going.

Anna was sorry when the evening ended, and the Laine family went home.

Chapter Fourteen

After the holidays, life quickly settled into an everyday pattern. Anna was back at school. Mother and Liisa looked after the cow and chickens. After school, Anna carried wood for the cook stove. Liisa and Mother brought in the wood for the heater. The logs were too big for Anna to handle.

The days were gradually getting a little longer, but several times the temperature fell to forty-below and lower. Those nights Mother insisted that Anna and Liisa both come into bed with her.

"I'll have to get up during the night to keep the fires going, but even then I'd be scared that you will freeze alone in your beds."

On the worst morning, when they woke up the water in the pail was frozen. Mother had to break the ice before she could get water for coffee and for porridge.

"You aren't going to school today, Anna. You'll freeze your face before you get to the road. Just stay in bed for now, both of you, I'll get this place warmed up. I will have to make a fire in the chicken coop, if we still have chickens and they're not all frozen."

Anna could hear Mother going out. She fell asleep again, snuggled against Liisa.

When she woke up, she was alone in bed and she could hear Mother and Liisa talking in the kitchen. She could smell coffee. Just then Mother poked her head into the bedroom. "I didn't mean that you should sleep all day. Come, the kitchen is warm, and the porridge is ready. Bring your clothes with you."

The kitchen was warm but it seemed darker than usual even though it was nearly eleven o'clock. Then Anna noticed the windows. They were thickly frosted with a regular forest of frosty flowers, leaves, branches. At the top of the window the icy edges were beginning to melt a little, like candles dripping.

"It's bitter cold out there. I don't think I've ever seen weather this cold before," Mother said.

"You haven't spent a winter in this bush before," Liisa retorted.

"That's true," Mother said quietly.

Anna was glad she didn't say anything more.

Anna enjoyed the day, except that she was a little upset when Mother wouldn't let her go out at all. She wouldn't even let her carry the wood. "The path is all blown in and you wouldn't be able to move fast enough to keep warm. You better stay inside."

The nicest part of the day came in the late afternoon when Korpi-seta came and brought them mail. The post office was eight miles away and various members of the community took turns in bringing it to a box at Moving Post corner.

There was a letter from Father! They hadn't heard from him since just before Christmas, a couple of weeks after he had gone to the bush camp. He had even a short note for Anna.

He was working hard and he was pleased with the amount of pulpwood he was able to cut each day. The conditions at the camp were fair, although in this exceptionally cold weather the walls were all frosty so that if any clothes were left touching the wall they would be stuck tight in the morning. The cooks were Finnish so they had stews and soups which he said was better than pork and beans all the time. In Anna's letter, he said he was lonely for them and was looking forward to the day when he could come home.

"How long is Father going to stay there?" Anna asked Mother.

"Another month and a half. He'll be home some time in March, depending on the weather."

"That's going to be such a long time," Anna complained.

"Yes, it is a long time," Mother sighed.

Chapter Fifteen

It was a few nights later that they first heard the wolves.

Anna was already in bed, but still awake when she heard the chorus of shivery howling. She thought first of dogs. *But there's only one dog at Laine's, and Korpi's have one—they couldn't make all that noise.* Then she remembered the stories she had heard grown-ups tell in Finland of packs of wolves coming from the great Russian forests. She shivered. *Those must be wolves.* Then she heard Mother and Liisa in the kitchen.

Liisa was crying, "This is the kind of country Father brought us into—wilderness, frozen wilderness, and now we are surrounded by wild beasts."

Mother made some soothing sounds, but Liisa sobbed even louder.

Anna wished Father were home. He would not be afraid. He would know what to do. She finally fell asleep as she concentrated on Father coming home.

In the morning when Anna got up, Liisa was still asleep, and when she walked into the kitchen, she was surprised to see the lamp still lit, even though it was already dawn. The kitchen was warm and Mother was sitting in a chair with her eyes closed.

As Anna walked towards her, she opened her eyes and stared at Anna as if she didn't know where she was.

"Voi, voi, Anna, how late is it? How long have I slept?" She did not explain why she was in her clothes from the night before and why she was sitting in the chair sleeping. She just began her morning tasks, making porridge, coffee, and getting ready for milking.

"I'm glad it is Saturday and you don't have to go to school," she said as she left for the barn.

Anna knew she was still thinking of the wolves. She tried to listen for the wolf sounds but could only hear the crackling of the fire in the stove, and the blowing of the wind against the windows.

Liisa came into the kitchen after Mother left. Her eyes were all red and she said nothing to Anna as she helped herself to coffee and porridge. And Anna didn't dare talk to her for fear she'd start crying again as she had the evening before.

Anna felt scared and alone. She tried to concentrate on her breakfast, making her porridge into little mountains and milk valleys, flat fields and milk rivers.

Then even worse things seemed to be happening.

Mother came back from the barn looking distraught and agitated.

"Did you see a wolf, Aiti?"

"Wh . . . what? Oh . . . no I didn't. Something worse has happened," Mother said.

Anna couldn't imagine what something worse would be. Maybe the wolves had gotten into the barn.

"Liisa," Mother said, "will you go to Korpi's and ask him to come right away, if he can? He might know what to do."

"What is the matter?" Liisa demanded.

"Mustikki is sick. She wouldn't eat and she stands there rocking herself from one side to another as if in pain. Her sides are all hard and bulging."

"She'll get better," Anna hugged Mother around the waist.

"I hope so," Mother patted her on the shoulder. "But if Mustikki dies we won't have any milk, cream, or butter and I haven't any money to spare to buy any even if the neighbors had any to sell. And what is worse, when your father comes, we'll have to use some of his hard earned money to buy a cow, instead of getting a horse."

Even though it was only a half mile to Korpis, it seemed hours before Liisa came back. Mother kept going back and forth between the barn and the house.

"What did he say? Is he coming? How come he isn't with you?" Mother was full of questions even before Liisa was barely in the door.

"He's not coming," Liisa said. Before she could continue Mother burst into wailing.

"Not coming? Voi, voi, what will I do? What will I do?"

"Aiti, Aiti—you didn't let me finish," Liisa said impatiently.

Mother quieted and looked at Liisa.

"Korpi-seta is going to get a man who knows about animals. He's had veterinary training in the Old Country. He lives out Tarmola way, about five miles towards town. Korpi-seta is taking his horse and sleigh because the old man doesn't have a horse and is too old to ski."

"Thank heavens. That is wonderful."

It was mid-afternoon before they arrived. Anna saw them first, coming up the lane. "There they are," she called to her mother.

Mother had her coat on and was out the door before Anna could say anything more. "Set the table for coffee," she called before she closed the door.

Anna watched out of the window as the sleigh reached the yard. The man with Korpi-seta was bent over and he had a long beard. He had trouble getting out of the sleigh and when he bent over to get his bag, he had to support himself on the sideboard of the sleigh. Anna could see Mother shaking hands with both men and then leading them into the barn. She stood by the window, watching and waiting for them all to come out.

Poor Mustikki, she thought, *I hope it doesn't hurt too much,* and she tried to imagine the barn without her big, warm black sides, her brown eyes, and the tinkling of her bell as she chewed her cud.

Finally the barn door opened, but only Mother came out carrying some kind of bottle.

"Is Mustikki going to get well?" Anna and Liisa asked in unison.

"I don't know for sure," Mother was busy adding lukewarm water into the bottle that had some kind of white stuff at the bottom. Then she shook it vigorously. "Liisa, you can start the coffee now. We should be in soon," she said, as she left.

They came inside after what seemed a long time to Anna. She tried to look at their faces for any sign telling her about Mustikki.

"Please sit down," Mother said as she poured coffee into two cups. She did not sit down herself. "Please have some sandwiches." She hovered between the table and the stove.

Anna sat on the woodbox and watched the old man and the way his beard wiggled as he chewed on his sandwich. A couple of times his very bright blue eyes, that were partly hidden under the bushy eyebrows and his long hair, lighted on Anna. "What does the little flicka know? How do you like living in the Canadian woods?"

Anna just smiled. The old man did not really expect an answer.

When they finished eating they sat for a little while and talked about Finland. It turned out that the old man's parish was close to Mother's. They even knew some of the same people. But the old man had been in Canada for a long time.

Mother suddenly changed the subject, as if she had just remembered something.

"Korpi, did you hear the wolves howling last night? They were so loud here that I was sure they were going to come right into the house. I was scared to go out this morning."

"Yes, I heard them. They were certainly making a lot of noise. But you don't have to be afraid of them. They are the small kind, nothing like the wolves you hear about in the Finnish wilderness," Korpi-seta explained.

"Oh, what a relief. Did you hear what Korpi-seta said?" Mother looked at Anna and Liisa. Then she turned to the men. "We were all so frightened last night. They sounded so dangerous."

"I agree, they sound bad, but they are actually afraid of humans," Korpi-seta explained again.

The old man nodded in agreement. "That's true. I've never heard that they attack humans. In fact, I often wonder about those wolf stories we used to hear in the Old Country." He stood up. "We must get going. Thank you for the sandwiches and coffee."

At that Mother hurried into her bedroom where Anna knew she kept her money. Mother came out with a dollar bill and some change.

"How much do I owe?" she asked the old man.

"Oh, I don't know. You are new settlers."

"I don't want you coming all this way for nothing," Mother insisted and handed him the dollar.

"For sure I don't want this much. A half of that will do, if you insist." Mother put fifty cents on the table in front of him.

"I am so thankful that you were able to come. It would have been disastrous for us to lose that cow. Thank you very much." Then she turned to Korpi-seta and offered him some money, Anna couldn't see how much. But he, almost angrily, pushed away her hand, "You are neighbors, and neighbors help each other in this new land," he said, as he started towards the door.

"You are good. You have lost almost a day's work. Thank you, thank you," Anna could see that Mother was close to tears.

"Mustikki must be all right," Anna decided.

Chapter Sixteen

Mustikki did get well. By the next morning she was eating and drinking normally. Mother was happy. "Mustikki means a lot to us. We would have a very thin diet without her."

When Anna went into the barn that day, she patted Mustikki's face and talked to her, "You are a good cow. I'm glad you are feeling better." Mustikki just looked at her and then shook her bell.

The days were lengthening and even though the snow was still deep, there was a change in the air—a lightness and a brightness. Some days after school Anna walked around the yard and on the bare rocks along hillside. She liked the sound of her boots on the rock and it was exciting to see the bare ground where the snow had edged away from the sun-warmed rocks and tree trunks. *Spring is coming, spring is coming, Isa will be home* was the refrain that kept going through her head.

But there were still days and weeks ahead before Father would be home. When Anna asked Mother the fourth time one Saturday, when Father would be home, she became impatient. "I don't want to hear any more from you about Father. Father has to stay as long as it is necessary and as long as the work lasts. Don't talk about it anymore."

Anna felt more miserable than ever. She was lonely for Father and now Mother shouted at her. *Didn't she care when Father came home?* She put on her coat, hat, and mitts.

"Where are you going?" asked Mother.

"Outside," she said as she ran out the door.

The day was overcast and gray. *The whole world is lonely because Father isn't here*, she thought as she kicked the hard pieces of snow along the path. She wished she could go and visit some of her favorite places, but the snow was too deep. She had tried earlier in the winter. There was a funny shaped birch tree with a branch sticking out, on which it was nice to sit; there was a sort of cave made by big rocks leaning against each other; there was a group of jackpines that made a nice shadowy place, where she could pick the funny curved cones. In the summer and fall, she used to visit these places regularly. Because of her misery she thought she'd try again. Maybe some of the snow had melted. To her surprise she did not not sink into the snow when she stepped off the path. She found she could walk on top of the snow!

Anna took a few more steps. It was like walking on a white pavement. It was wonderful. Here she was almost on level with the fence posts. She walked and walked, around and around the clearing. Then she tried running. The snow held her. She ran and ran. She was no longer confined to paths. She felt much happier. When she was tired of running she decided to go to the crooked birch. She climbed up to her favorite branch and sat and looked around. The day seemed brighter and she could feel the wind on her face. Clouds behind the house and over the hill were beginning to thin out. A chickadee in the next tree chittered to her, as if to say that spring is really coming.

Chapter Seventeen

That evening she had already gone to bed but she wasn't asleep. Mother and Liisa were still in the kitchen. It was a cold night and the moon was nearly full. Anna looked at the moon which she could see from her bed. *It does look as if has a face,* she thought and she began to recite a memory work verse from her Reader, *Lady Moon, Lady Moon where are you roving?* when suddenly she heard a noise. She thought at first it was a wolf howling and she pushed herself down deeper into the bed clothes, as she always did when she heard them. But as the sounds came again, she knew this was something different, something more frightening. Anna could hear Mother's and Liisa's voices through the doorway.

"What's that noise?" Liisa said.

"Wolves," Mother answered.

"No, no—listen," Liisa insisted.

Anna could hear them opening the door.

"What on earth?" Mother exclaimed as the sounds came louder.

Anna jumped out of bed and ran into the kitchen. An icy blast of air hit her.

"Get back into bed," Mother commanded. "Close the door Liisa. I'll put my coat on. It sounds like someone's in trouble."

Anna went back in her room but not into bed. She looked out of the window facing the road. At first, she could only see the yard and clearing glimmering in the moonlight and the woods beyond, dark and in Anna's imagination, full of wolves. But then she saw the flames, and the dark forms coming up the lane. A terrible fear shook her—that was Helmi's home on fire. She watched as the flames leapt high and then she could hardly see them, only black smoke boiled up, and again the flames rose sending off sparks into the night. She could hear the voices closer now, the dark figures were coming into the yard. She recognized the high wailing voice as Helmi's mother's. She could hear Mother calling to them and the door opening. Anna was afraid to look into the kitchen for fear of what she would or would not find. Was Helmi with them or was she inside those leaping flames, or was someone else missing? She remembered hearing stories about a child who had burned somewhere not too far away, she wasn't sure just where. She turned around and walked slowly to the doorway of the kitchen and just stood there. There was great commotion as Helmi's mother, Elsa, Aili, Lily, and Helmi all stood in the middle of the kitchen floor. They were all crying except for Lily who was just staring wide-eyed as if still asleep.

Helmi's mother, Laine-tati, was talking and crying. Her voice was squeaky and broken.

"I . . . I don't, don't know wh . . . what happened. All of a sudden the f . . . f . . . fire was just there, a . . . ar . . . around the kitchen stove pipes, flaming. The girls." She stopped and hugged them all. "The g . . . g . . . girls were sleeping in the kitchen with me because it was so cold. Wh . . . what if they had been in the attic, they would never have gotten away. They would have all burnt . . . voi, voi, voi." And she began to cry louder than ever.

Mother tried to lead her to a chair, "Seliina, Seliina. They didn't burn. Your children are all here. Come sit down. Liisa, there's some hot water in the kettle, make some tea, and girls, sit down—Elsa, take Lily into your lap. Anna get a blanket from your bed . . . Elsa wrap your sister in it."

Anna's mother was trying to make order out of chaos.

Anna brought a blanket to Elsa who wrapped her little sister into it and cradled her in her arms, swaying back and forth. Helmi took refuge with her sister Aili. Anna looked at them and felt almost as if they were strangers—even Helmi.

Mother succeeded in dragging Laine-tati to a chair by the table. Then she leaned over and hugged her, "I tell you, your children are safe."

But again Laine-tati began to lament, "Voi, voi, voi. What will Kalle say. Everything is gone . . . all our clothes, some of his tools . . . we'll have to start all over again. His winter's work in the bush will be for nothing. We were going to buy a horse and a cow and, maybe even build a house. We had so many plans." She continued crying in great breathless gulps.

Anna was frightened. She had never heard grown-ups crying like this, not even at funerals.

Mother continued to stand by Laine-tati and hold her until Liisa brought the tea. "Try to drink this. It will at least warm you up," Mother coaxed.

For a few moments the kitchen was quiet and Anna could hear only the crackling in the stove and the cup clinking into the saucer.

Laine-tati's voice was quieter as she asked Mother: "How will I get hold of Kalle? I think I remember the address, but that's for the office in town."

"I think if we speak to Korpi, he will go to that address and give a message. I'm sure that in a case like this something can be done. But now, after you have finished your tea, we better think of getting some sleep. We can do nothing tonight anymore. It's midnight. In the morning, the girls can go to Korpi's, at least Liisa can."

I have to try to remember that it could have been much worse," Laine-tati said.

Mother continued her organizing: "About beds—you Seliina, and Lily can sleep with me. I think Helmi will fit with Anna, but Liisa's bed is too narrow for anyone else. We'll make a bed for you older girls here beside the stove. I have an old comforter and we'll use coats to cover you. At your age, you should still be able to sleep on anything. First, let's get Lily into bed. Anna you take Helmi into yours."

For the first time, Anna really looked at Helmi. She still had her coat over her nightgown and her boots pulled over her bare feet. Her hair was coming out of her braids and her eyes were red from crying. Anna suddenly felt that she wanted to hug her but felt too shy, She took Helmi's hand and brought her into the bedroom. Mother came in after them and bustled fixing up the blankets.

"I think it will be easier if you sleep with your heads in the opposite ends. This cot is quite long. Your feet will just touch when you're stretched out. Anna you climb in first and then Helmi. I'll cover you carefully."

Anna could feel Helmi's feet but neither said anything to the other as they lay in the cot. Anna did not at all feel sleepy and would liked to have talked, but did not know what to say. They couldn't chatter about any ordinary things and so she remained quiet. Soon she could hear Helmi breathing regularly; Anna lay awake for awhile longer. The light in the kitchen was blown out as Mother went to bed after she had settled Elsa and Aili. She could hear Mother and Laine-tati talking quietly. She finally fell asleep.

Chapter Eighteen

Anna woke up in the morning to voices in the kitchen. It took her awhile to sort out the night's happenings. She could feel Helmi at her feet and the memory of the leaping flames made her want to stay in bed. She heard Mother talking to Laine-tati.

"I think it's best that Helmi go to school with Anna this morning. I think I can find something from Anna's clothes for her."

"I guess so—I don't know—maybe you are right, maybe it would be best. She does have her overcoat and boots. If you can find stockings, underwear, and some kind of dress, she can go." Anna could hear tears in Laine-tati's voice.

A little later Mother came into the bedroom. "Wake up girls. It's time to get ready for school."

Anna and Helmi giggled as Mother tried some of Anna's clothes on Helmi. Helmi was smaller and looked lost in some of them. Mother finally found a skirt and sweater that fit fairly well.

Anna noticed that Laine-tati was wearing one of Mother's dresses, but Aili and Elsa were still in their night clothes. Anna decided that Liisa's clothes would be too large for them and hers too small.

While Anna and Helmi were having breakfast, there was a knock at the door, startling everyone because it was so early. It was Maki-seta from up the road and his first words were, when he saw the Laines, "Thank God, you are all here. I was scared to look into the ruins of your sauna for fear of what I'd find there. I hoped that you had all gotten away. You are all safe?" He looked around again. "Where is the little one?" His voice rose sharply.

Laine-tati didn't answer, she looked as if she was going to cry. Mother hurried to assure him, "Lily is fast asleep in our bed. Yes, thank God, they are all safe," she added.

"But we wouldn't all be here if the girls had been sleeping upstairs in the loft," Laine-tati launched into a long detailed explanation of why they weren't.

Mother cut in to ask if Maki-seta wanted coffee but he refused, "I'm going into town and I want to get back home before dark. I came in just to find out about the Laines."

"You're going into town?" Mother perked up, "Maybe you could go to the timber company office and ask them to send a message to Laine."

"Yes, sure, I can do that. What is the company?"

Aili answered before her mother got herself together. "It's the Northern Timber Company."

"Good, I know where that is. I worked for them one year."

"So you'll do that?" Mother asked again.

"Sure, sure," Maki answered.

"Good, then we don't have to send a message to Korpi. You might stop at their place, since you're going right by, to tell them what happened. Maybe they might have some clothes for Elsa and Aili."

"Sure, I'll stop by their place, but why don't you go and see my wife. She would be glad to help. She could ski around the countryside and tell other people."

"That's an idea. We have to do something." Mother looked at the clock. "Anna and Helmi, you two better get going or you're going to be late."

At school Helmi and Anna felt a curious importance as they told the teacher and others about the fire. Some of the older boys rushed over to the burn site and came back with a twisted mass of metal, that had been a tea kettle and some smaller pieces that were melted down cutlery.

"See Helmi, you can't boil water in that anymore. How about trying to eat with these spoons," Aarne said to her.

Helmi just stared at them but did not say anything. Anna was afraid Helmi might start crying. She didn't. She just stared wide-eyed at the objects.

"Aarne, what is the matter with you," the teacher scolded. "Take those things outside this minute, do you hear me?"

Anna could see that the teacher was upset and angry.

But the arithmetic, the reading, and the geography lessons went along as if nothing had happened. When Anna looked at Helmi in her borrowed clothes, she wondered how the lessons could be the same after such a terrible night. But the day dragged on and Helmi remained calm until it was time to go home, when she announced that she would stay at school. No matter what Anna said, she just kept on repeating, "I'm going to stay here."

"You can't stay here," Anna was bewildered and close to tears. All the other children were gone, only the teacher was working at her desk. She looked up, "What's the problem?" she asked.

"Helmi doesn't want to come with me. Her mother and her sisters are at my place. She is supposed to come with me," Anna was desperate.

The teacher tried to talk to her but it wasn't until she said she'd come with them that Helmi began to move. She put on her coat, hat, and mitts.

"Just a minute," the teacher said, as she went into her place at the back of the school. Soon she came out with a bright red and yellow blanket, and some pretty dress material. "I haven't very much here but maybe you can use this blanket and this material. I was going to sew it into a suit for myself, but maybe you and your sisters can use it. It should be enough for a skirt for each.

Helmi's eyes opened wide as she stared at the material and the blanket, and for the first time Anna saw her smile a little.

When they got to Anna's the kitchen was full of people and there was a pile of clothing, bed clothes, pots, pans, and dishes in one corner. Anna knew some of the people, but many were strangers. They had all come to bring something for the Laines. Mother and Liisa were serving coffee. The room quieted when the teacher and the girls walked in. They all watched as the teacher walked over to Laine-tati and handed her the blanket and the dress material.

"I'm so sorry about the fire. Here are a couple of things you might be able to use."

Laine-tati just smiled and kept saying, "Kiitos, Kiitos," over and over again.

Some of the talk started again, but in lower voices. Mother set a clean cup and saucer on the table. She touched the teacher on the shoulder and then pointed to the chair. She turned to Anna and asked her to invite the teacher for coffee. Anna felt suddenly shy, but she obeyed her mother.

"Mother says, please sit down and have some coffee."

The teacher looked at Mother and said, "Thank you. I will enjoy a cup of coffee."

"Helmi and Anna, you sit down too," Mother said. Some of the others had left the table when the teacher sat down. "So the teacher won't be alone."

The girls, although they felt shy, enjoyed sitting with the teacher, drinking their milk and coffee and eating pulla and cake. The teacher talked to them as if they were grown-ups. It reminded Anna of the time of the big storm, when there were only four pupils at school and the teacher seemed so different.

When they finished, the teacher shook hands with Mother and thanked her and then she talked to Laine-tati again telling her she was sorry about the fire; both Mother and Laine-tati nodded and smiled.

Laine-tati kept repeating, "kiitos, kiitos."

After everyone left, Mother and Laine-tati began to look through all the stuff that was piled up.

"This will give you a bit of a start," Mother remarked.

"Yes, yes," Laine-tati said. "Such good neighbors in this new country."

Chapter Nineteen

It was the fourth morning after the fire. Anna and Helmi were having breakfast with Aili and Elsa, Liisa was kneading bread dough, and Mother had just finished sieving milk into the creamer and was washing up the milk pail and the sieve. Laine-tati was sitting by the stove with a coffee cup, staring at the floor.

"When Kalle comes we'll have to do something. We can't be in your way here forever."

"I wish you would stop worrying about it. Just until you get something built on your own land isn't exactly forever," Mother's voice was impatient, as it sometimes was when Anna said something silly.

"I suppose we could stay in that same shack we lived in before we moved to our own place. We do have food—it's lucky we stored our flour, sugar, and other dry foods in the little outside shack and we have meat hanging there, but it would be so far to come to feed the chickens and milk the cows."

Mother turned around suddenly and looked at Laine-tati, "I just thought of something. When Kalle comes home, why don't you move into our sauna. It's not the greatest place in the world but we lived in it for a few months and Eino lived there over the winter and there's our old cook stove in it, and you now have all these household goods the neighbors have brought. There you could be in peace with your own family." Mother walked over to her, took her by the shoulders and shook her gently, "In fact you could stay there until spring and Kalle could go back to work and make a little more money. I know how much that money they earn in the bush means to all of us."

"How can we ever repay you," Laine-tati said and burst into tears.

"Nonsense. Don't talk like that. We are all from the Old Country trying to make a new life in this new land," Mother scolded.

"Maybe we would have been better off staying in our torppa in Finland," Laine-tati started talking almost as if to herself. "But Kalle was so determined to get his own land. He always said he'd never get it in Finland. Sometimes I'm so homesick, I can hardly stand it. I'll never see my mother or my sisters and brothers again."

Anna could see that Laine-tati's face was twisting in silent crying. Even Mother looked sad and Liisa, just finishing the bread dough, got that same angry look Anna had seen so many times.

Mother roused herself first. "Don't you think it's a good idea?" Mother asked again referring to the sauna. But she did not wait for an answer because she suddenly realized how late it was. "For goodness sake girls. Look at the clock. If you don't hurry, you'll be late for school. Come, come, get your coats, hurry," she hustled Anna and Helmi out of the door into the cold morning.

When they got back home in the afternoon, Anna was surprised to see their kitchen back to normal. Helmi's family had already moved into the sauna dressing room. Mother explained as they were having their pulla and coffee, "The girls went right down this morning, made a fire in the cookstove, heated water and scrubbed out the place. Maki came later and hammered together a couple of cots and then he went around and got some more bedding from the neighbors." Then Mother turned to Helmi, "and we have even a bigger surprise for you." Before the girls had time to say anything, there was a knock at the door.

"Come in," Mother called.

There was Helmi's father.

"Isa!" Helmi cried.

"Good, there you are Helmi. Now I believe that all my family is safe," Laine-seta said.

Helmi was all smiles.

Anna felt a twinge of jealousy. Helmi got her father back while her father was still away.

"Will you have a cup of coffee and some pulla, Kalle?" Mother asked.

"No, no, Seliina wondered if you could give us a little salt. I'll be going into town tomorrow to pick up a few things."

"Of course, why didn't I think of it." Mother put some salt into a little jar and handed it to Laine-seta.

"Put your coat on Helmi." Laine-seta did not speak to Anna, which was unusual. He was one grown-up who always noticed her and made some kind of joke. Anna felt let down. Even Helmi just went off with her father without saying anything to her.

That evening the house seemed unnaturally quiet after all the commotion of the past few days. They sat around the lamplit table, Mother knitting, Liisa embroidering, and Anna doing her homework. The fire crackled in the stove and the kettle murmured gently.

"I just remembered that today is Friday, mail day, but Korpi hasn't brought our mail as he usually does."

Just as Mother finished saying this, they heard skis being lifted against the wall and footsteps on the step.

"Come in," Mother called in answer to the knock at the door.

It was Korpi-seta and he had an armful of mail for them. There was Eaton's summer catalogue that Liisa grabbed first. Mother got a letter from Mummo in Finland as well as some magazines, but the best bit of mail was a letter from Father.

As Mother was reading it, both Anna and Liisa kept repeating, "What does he say? What does he say? When is he coming home?"

Anna could tell from Mother's face that the news was good. Her cheeks became pink and she was smiling. She looked at the calendar. "When is the twenty eighth? It's next Wednesday," she turned to look at the girls. "Your father is coming home next Wednesday."

"Let's see, let's see," Liisa wanted to look at the letter.

"Don't you believe me?" Mother laughed. "Don't tear it. Here." She let Liisa take the letter as she continued, "he's getting into town early Wednesday morning, and he expects to be home some time in the afternoon."

Anna tried to peak at the letter over Liisa's shoulder. What wonderful news! But how could she ever wait until next Wednesday. Five days! That was going to take forever.

"What's this surprise he talks about at the end of the letter?" Liisa asked.

"I don't know. I guess we just have to wait to find out," Mother kept smiling.

Chapter Twenty

The next five days were the longest Anna had ever lived. She thought Wednesday would never come. When it finally came, she wanted to stay home from school. She couldn't see how she could sit in school all day wondering if Father had come. But Mother wouldn't hear of it.

"He says in his letter, he's coming in the afternoon. Who knows what time in the afternoon. More likely not until after you get home. I'm not going to have you here moping all day. No, you better go to school."

She went off reluctantly. During the day the teacher had to speak to her several times because she was not paying attention.

"What's gotten into you Anna? You are usually not like this."

The day dragged to four o'clock. Anna could hardly button her coat because her fingers trembled so. Usually she and Helmi were the last to leave but this afternoon she hurried out of the school by herself. When she got out of the school gate, she ran down the hill as fast as she could. She did not want anyone to catch up to her. She was past the Moving Post crossroads and over the next hill before she slowed down. She could hear her moccasins squeaking on the snow and she saw a Canada Jay on a nearby branch looking at her. She paid no attention to the little creek at which she and Helmi usually played, breaking off the lacy bits of ice that clung to the sides of the culvert. Maybe Father was home already. He said Wednesday afternoon, and this was Wednesday afternoon.

Just as she got to the curve of the long hill that ended near her home gate, she heard the jingling of the harness and the creak of the sleigh behind her.

It's Maki-seta, she thought, but as she looked back, she could see that the horse was light brown and much smaller than Maki's black horse. She stepped off the road and waited for it to pass. Maybe it belonged to the new people who lived on the side road from the next crossing.

"Anna, I looked for you among the other children but I didn't see you. Did you get off earlier that you're way up here."

Anna couldn't believe her eyes or ears. It was Father! She just stood at the side of the road and didn't move.

"Come girl, don't just stand there. Don't you know your own father?" He was laughing, delighted to be able to surprise her in this way.

Anna looked at the horse and she looked at the sleigh and again at Father, and she began to smile, but she still stood without moving.

"Is that our horse and sleigh?" she asked.

"Yes, yes. Isn't he nice? Come girl, come. You're lucky, You'll be the first one, except me, to get a ride with our brand new horse and sleigh," Father said as he put out his hand to help her get up beside him.

"Giddap," he said to the horse and shook the reins. As the horse and sleigh began to move, Anna looked up at Father and he put his arm around her and said, "You've grown in these three months. How has everything been with you, Liisa, and Aiti?"

"Fine," she just said. She couldn't tell him how much they had all missed him. She knew too, that her father had missed them, but he wouldn't say much about it.

"His name is Bobby," Father said suddenly. He was talking about the horse.

It was funny to hear him say the English name. It didn't sound quite right coming from him. He made a long 'aw' sound from the 'o'.

"Bobby?" Anna repeated, but as a question. "Is that what we are going to call him and not a Finnish name?"

"It's the name he is used to. He is a Canadian horse. I have to talk to him in the ways of this country. He wouldn't understand if I talked to him in the way of the Old Country," Father explained.

By this time they were at their own gate. Father pulled on the rein to direct Bobby into the lane. There was still quite a bit of snow on the lane with only a path and a ski trail leading up to the yard.

"We'll see how he operates in the snow," Father said, more to himself then to Anna. The horse balked a little at some of the drifts but on Father's urging they soon were in the yard and at the kitchen door.

"You go in and tell your mother and Liisa to come out," Father said to Anna.

Mother was just taking bread from the oven and Liisa was peeling potatoes when Anna burst in.

"Well! You're home early," Mother commented.

"Come outside, come outside, come see the surprise," Anna shouted in her excitement.

"Close the door," Mother commanded. "What are you talking about? Close the door."

"Come outside, both you and Liisa," Anna stamped her feet in exasperation.

"See what? What's gotten into you?"

"Just come, you will see." She took Mother and Liisa by the hand and pulled them towards the door.

"Voi, voi—for goodness sake, Eino! Whose horse have you got?" Mother cried out.

"Is that all you can say when your husband comes home? This is our horse. Whose else would it be? Isn't he handsome?" Father got off the sleigh and walked to pat the horse's face. "Look," he said to the horse. "There's your family. You are part of the household now. His name is Bobby."

They all laughed when the horse rubbed his head on Father's shoulder, as if in answer to his introduction. Then they all patted the white triangle on his head. To Anna it looked as if he was taking a good look at them.

"Where are you going to keep him?" Mother asked.

"There's that shed beside the barn. He will be alright in there most days. There shouldn't be any really cold nights any more, but if there are we can always put him in with Mustikki."

Anna followed Father around as he unharnessed Bobby and led him into the shed, gave him a pail of water, and left a pan of oats and a pile of hay in front of him.

Mother and Liisa had supper on the table when she and Father came in. The house smelled of fresh bread and all the other good things Mother had made. It was almost like a Christmas meal—instead of ham they had venison Korpi-seta had given them, carrot and beet salad, a turnip loaf, and mashed potatoes, and rice pudding with raspberry sauce for dessert. Anna felt it was Christmas when they all sat around the table and Father told them stories about his winter. Anna felt warm and happy.

Long after the table was cleared, the dishes done, and Anna was lying on her cot, she could hear Mother and Father still talking, making plans. Anna heard them talk of going into town for a day, now that they had their own horse and sleigh.

"But what we really need is a cutter in which to get around. Going with the big sleigh will be slow," Father was saying.

Mother's voice answered, "Don't get ahead of yourself, Eino. We can't afford that now. You know that. We'll have to save enough money for a wagon for when the snow goes. The horse won't help much in the late spring and summer if we don't have a wagon."

"You're right. One thing at a time. We can cover the sleigh with hay and cover that with a blanket, and it will be comfortable enough for all of us," Father conceded.

"Of course it will be. Let's go on Saturday. Maybe we can stop in at Perttula's. I haven't had a chance to talk to Saimi properly since last summer." Mother sounded happy.

"Yes, let's go. There are things I'll need for jobs around here and we must be getting low on some of the basic groceries.

Hearing that, woke Anna right out of her drowsiness. For a long time she couldn't get to sleep because she kept thinking about the trip into town.

Chapter Twenty-One

Anna hated to go to school the next morning. She had to leave when Mother, Father, and Liisa were having their breakfast and laughing and talking around the table. But Mother wouldn't hear of her staying home for the day.

"It's not good for you to get the idea that you can stay home from school unless you are sick. No matter what you are doing, you have to learn to do faithfully."

Anna met Helmi half way down the hill where the path from the sauna joined the lane. Anna told her friend first thing, "My father came home yesterday and we have a horse and sleigh."

"My mother said she saw the horse and sleigh. It's nice to have your father at home," Helmi said politely. Her father had gone back to work a few days after the fire.

The day dragged in the schoolroom. She made the silliest mistakes in her arithmetic. Again the teacher scolded her, "What's happening to you Anna? You just don't seem to have your mind of your work."

"My father came home and we have a new horse," she blurted out even though she hadn't intended saying anything. She could hear sniggering from the side of the bigger pupils.

"Oh," the teacher said, "how long was your father away?"

"For three months."

"That's a long time. And you have a new horse. You will enjoy going for a sleigh ride, won't you," the teacher smiled at her.

"We are going to town on Saturday." Anna felt as if she couldn't control her tongue.

"That's exciting. No wonder you have difficulty keeping your mind on your work. But you will have to try. You have to get through tomorrow yet. Maybe if you concentrate on your work the time will go faster," the teacher laid her hand on Anna's shoulder and gave it a little squeeze.

Anna didn't know if the teacher's advice worked or not, but Saturday morning did come. After the chores, they started getting ready. They had to dress warmly and take extra covers for the sleigh.

The journey seemed to take forever and Anna kept asking, "Are we there soon?"

Mother told her to go to sleep. "We still have a long way to go." She covered Anna with an extra blanket. "Go to sleep. You were up early. It'll do you good."

When Anna woke up, the sleigh was stopped in front of Perttula's house.

"Wake up, Anna," Liisa was saying to her. "We're in town."

Anna sat up, a little dazed, not quite sure what was happening. She looked about her. They were on a street with small houses along both sides. Perttula's was a white house with a little front porch.

"Wait a minute, don't get out yet. I will go and see if they are at home," Mother said. "If they're not, we will have to go and do our business first and then come back. I know that Saimi works a few days a week housecleaning but I don't know what days."

Anna saw Saimi-tati opening the door and heard her voice exclaiming, "For goodness sake, Eeva. I'm so glad to see you. I thought you had disappeared into the Canadian woods forever. Come in, come in, you must be famished. Oh, thank you, thank you." She took a jar of cream that Mother was unwinding from an old green scarf.

Then Mother turned around and called: "Come girls, Eino."

Liisa and Anna hurried to the door but Father said he'd feed Bobby first.

Anna looked around Perttula's house. It seemed to so fine to her. The door led first to the parlor where there was a sofa and a very shiny table centered with a small embroidered cloth. There was a pretty rug partly covering the floor; the rest of the floor was a shiny brown.

Anna wondered where their daughter, Lillian, was but she was too shy to ask. Lillian was the same age as Anna and she had been friendly to Anna the summer before. Saimi-tati hurried to make coffee and sandwiches for them which she served at a table in the sunny kitchen. And all the time she and Mother talked. Father finally said: "If we are to get all our buying done and get home in time to milk and feed Mustikki, we better get going. You two could go on for days."

"That's true Eino. Why can't Eeva and the girls stay here for a couple of days. You can always come back for them," Saimi-tati looked at Anna. "Anna did not even see Lillian. She should be home soon."

But before Father could say anything, Mother answered.

"No, no—we have to get back home, but when nice weather comes, maybe you can get out to see us and then we will probably come into town more often, now that we have our own horse."

Saimi-tati was letting them out of the door when suddenly she exclaimed, "There's Lillian, coming up the street now. Anna, why don't you stay and play here while your parents do their errands. They can pick you up afterwards. You won't like running around town with them. You could stay too, Liisa."

Saimi-tati was very insistent.

Liisa shook her head emphatically, but Anna was torn between the excitement of going into the stores with Mother and Father, and staying and playing with this town girl.

"That is up to Anna, whatever she wants to do," Mother said.

Anna just stood and looked from one to the other.

Father was impatiently waiting on the sleigh. Liisa had already climbed in, but Mother stood waiting beside Saimi-tati.

"Come on Eeva, we have to get going. Anna, make up your mind," Father called.

Saimi-tati decided for her. She laid an arm across Anna's shoulders and her other on Lillian's and turned to go into the house. Mother called to her, "Be a good girl, Anna, we'll be back around four o'clock."

When they got back into the house and began to take off their coats, Saimi-tati brought a pair of knitted slippers for Anna. "Do you want to take off your boots? You will be more comfortable in these."

Anna felt shy and tongue-tied. She and Lillian hadn't said a word to each other.

Lillian had to have lunch, so Saimi-tati insisted that Anna eat again. Lillian finally started asking her questions as they were eating. She asked about school and what games they played. She spoke in English. Her mother looked at Anna. "Do you understand? Lillian forgets that you've been here only a few months."

Anna just nodded. She could understand most of what Lillian said.

But Lillian's reaction surprised Anna. "I hope she understands English. I can hardly understand Finnish any more."

Anna wondered how she talked to her parents if she couldn't speak Finnish, but she noticed later that most of the time Lillian answered her mother in English.

As they began to play, Lillian told Anna what to do, "You be Mrs. Hill, and I'll be Mrs. Brown. That's your house over there and mine is over here." She pointed to the corners of the bedroom. "Mine is a big fancy house, like some of those the Canadians have."

After a while they got tired of playing house and Lillian decided they should play store and she was the store lady and Anna was the customer. Anna watched fascinated as Lillian tried to act the part of a store lady. She held her lips pressed together, her hands fluttered over the toys that were the make-believe goods and every so often she patted her hair.

Then playing store was no longer fun. Lillian took out her paper dolls. "My friend from school who is a Canadian girl gave me these. She's really a nice girl. She never calls me a dirty Finn or a foreigner. She's very nice and so is her mother. I go to her house a lot. Her mother even lets her come to my house."

"What do you mean, a dirty Finn? We're not dirty," Anna was astonished.

"Oh, they don't mean really dirty with dirt. It's just a way of talking to us who are immigrants. I hate the word immigrant. It makes all of us sound dumb. Sometimes they chase us home and push us into the snow, and sometimes even worse things," she added darkly.

Anna was glad she didn't live in town and go to the school that Lillian went to.

Time went by quickly and Anna was surprised when Saimi-tati called them to have more to eat. "Your parents will be here soon, and you have a long trip home. Eat well. Have some meat and potatoes and carrots. After you finish that, I have some Canadian dessert for you.

Anna enjoyed the meal, but especially the dessert. It was cold and sweet, strawberry tasting stuff, and Saimi-tati had whipped some of the cream Mother had brought and spooned generous helpings over it.

They had just finished when Mother came to the door.

"Eeva, don't you have time to come in and have something to eat?" Saimi-tati asked.

"No, no. We have to get going. I have to get back to feed and milk the cow. And anyway we don't want to get caught in the dark. The house will be cold. Come hurry up Anna, Father and Liisa are waiting in the sleigh. Thank you very much, Saimi, for everything and for having Anna here."

Saimi-tati handed Mother the jar in which the cream had come, and another parcel, "There's some meat balls and a potato loaf that you can heat up when you get home."

"That's very thoughtful of you, but you shouldn't have troubled yourself so much," Mother said.

"No trouble, no trouble at all. It was good to see you, even for a short time," Saimi-tati said.

They were all quiet on the way home. Anna thought of Lillian's house—of the sofa in the nice parlor and the shiny floors, and she felt envious. But then she remembered Lillian's school and all those children of the other tongue who sometimes called you a dirty Finn. She decided that it was better in their own little school where everybody was the same. Even Aarne's and Olavi's taunts about being an Old Country dumb-bell seemed mild compared to what went on at Lillian's school.

Chapter Twenty-Two

Spring was coming. The melting snow was making rivers along the roadside—that's what Anna and Helmi called the melting run-offs. The two girls directed waters at will, made lakes and falls, main rivers and tributaries, regular landscapes along the hillside. They played for hours creating these new worlds. The rocks down towards the road were becoming bare and sounded nice and loud as they hopped and skipped on them.

Other things were happening. Helmi's new home was almost ready. Her father and brother were back home working on it. On Saturdays, Anna and Helmi had fun playing among the sweet smelling chips from the logs. And when Laine-tati stopped in for a visit, she did not cry all the time and Laine-seta had started teasing Anna again.

However, there were also upsetting things in Anna's life. Liisa had finally wrested permission from Father and Mother to look for a job in town. There had been great arguments, but Liisa got her way. But Mother insisted that Liisa not go into town to look for a job on her own. Instead, Mother wrote to Saimi-tati to ask if she knew of any place for Liisa. While waiting for an answer, Liisa was so absent minded and far away that Anna felt almost as if she had already left. When the letter came saying that she should come right away, Liisa became very talkative and lively. Saimi-tati said in her letter that a big house needed a girl for the kitchen and that the cook was Finnish.

"It will be a good place to get started and to learn the language," she wrote.

"Aren't you sorry now you didn't go to school with Anna? It would be much easier for you now to know some English," Father said to Liisa that evening.

"No, I couldn't have stood being there with the little kids. Aili and Elsa are younger and they could stand it only until Christmas. I'll be all right. The cook is Finnish. I don't need much English." Liisa tossed her head in a knowing way.

"That's no way to think," Father said.

"Why not? I'm not going to stay in this country. When I get enough money saved, I'm going back."

Mother and Father said nothing. Anna felt sad.

Liisa left the next day. She walked to Korpi's and from there got a ride into town with him.

"I'm glad Saimi is in town to keep an eye on her. She is so young and headstrong. It would be bad enough having her go if we were still at home, but to go into that unknown world of strangers of the other tongue—it scares me."

"I don't suppose it's any worse here than it is at home. She'd probably have to work harder at home. My sister worked for that silversmith's family. She had to carry water up a long hill and always work, work like a slave. But even so she will be busy enough. I understand they get Thursday afternoon off and the occasional evening. That won't give her much time to get into mischief. Anyway that's life. We all have to leave home," Father tried to comfort Mother.

"Do you think she is serious about going back?" Mother asked, after what seemed to Anna, a long, long silence.

"Maybe she is serious now, but lots of things can happen before she gets enough money together from a kitchen maid's pay," Father said.

That comforted Anna. At least Liisa wouldn't be leaving for Finland right away.

At school, everyone was beginning to talk about passing—whether or not they'd pass into the next grade. Anna and Helmi had moved to the First Reader at Christmas and they were now half way through it. The teacher had told them that if they worked hard and got through the First Reader, they could be in Junior Second in September and maybe by Christmas in Senior Second which would mean that they would be in the same grade in reading and arithmetic. The teacher's praise and encouragement made them both determined to get through the First Reader.

Then Mother had a note from Saimi-tati saying that they were planning on hiring a horse and carriage and coming out on the last Sunday of the month, when most of the snow was gone. If possible they would bring Liisa with them.

Mother was excited over the thought of having visitors, although she had some reservations. "Saimi has such a fancy house. She has a pretty parlor. I wonder what she will think of our peasant house with just a tupa—kitchen, parlor, dining room, all in one."

Father made a funny sound and said, "She'll like your cream alright. We're not going to get into any races with the city dwellers. We are farmers."

Anna was happy that Lillian would be coming. She was glad she had a nice store-bought doll. And anyway she could show her all the places she played in around the farm—the big rocks, crooked birch, the creek with little speckled trout, the pretend barn, and chicken coop under the big pine.

Anna was absent-minded with Helmi, as the Sunday when the visitors were to arrive approached. On the Friday before, she and Helmi had their first big quarrel and they walked home in silence. Anna told herself that she didn't care. Lillian was coming on Sunday and she would have a friend to play with.

On Sunday noon they finally saw a team pulling a carriage turning in at their lane.

"My, isn't that a nice carriage," Mother said, as it came into the yard.

"Nice horses," said Father.

But Anna could not see Lillian in the carriage. Mr. Perttula and Saimi-tati were in the front seat, but the person beside Liisa was not Lillian. It was some strange lady.

Anna felt altogether flattened. She fought against tears. She felt like running away to hide. But she couldn't, Mother would be too angry. Then she tried to concentrate on Liisa. She looked different; maybe it was the hat she was wearing, a high, flowered thing.

Saimi-tati started talking from the time the horse stopped and as she descended from the carriage.

"Eino, you've certainly brought Eeva a long way into the woods. Couldn't you find anything closer?"

Father just laughed and said, "The farther, the better."

"Voi, voi, Anna," Saimi-tati looked at her. "You waited for Lillian didn't you. Well, she was going to come until last evening when that Canadian friend of hers asked her to her place for the day. She just couldn't say no."

Anna stood as if stunned. *Of course*, she thought, *she had to go to her fancy friend.* She could not look at Saimi-tati for fear she'd start crying.

"That Liisa of ours has become a city person quickly," Father joked. "She doesn't even look like a little farm girl any more."

Liisa blushed and looked uncomfortable. Saimi-tati hastened to defend Liisa. "It's still the same Liisa. I gave her that spring hat because she had nothing appropriate to wear." Then Saimi-

92

tati turned to the strange woman. "Oh, pardon me, I'm letting you just stand there. Let me introduce Taimi Oja, Eeva and Eino Kallio, and this is Anna Kallio, Liisa's parents and sister. We asked Taimi to come for a ride when Lillian couldn't come."

"Or wouldn't," Anna said under her breath as she turned away.

"Come," Mother said, "come inside. I will have coffee ready in a few minutes."

Mother had set the table with her best linen cloth from Finland and Anna thought the plain white cups and plates with the little gold colored band looked quite nice on the cloth, but Liisa said quietly, so that only Mother and Anna could hear, "With my first pay I'm going to get you a table cloth from a store." Mother looked startled but did not say anything.

The visit was taken up mostly by Saimi-tati and Mother talking. They talked about being girls together in Finland. Saimi-tati talked about their life in town, about socials and dances they went to. Anna hardly had a chance to talk to Liisa, except when they were left alone to do the dishes when all the others went outside to look around the farm.

"Do you like working in town?" She asked her sister.

"Yes, I like it. The work is easy, not nearly as hard as it is here," Liisa said.

"Do you have to talk English?"

"How can I? I don't know any. Saimi-tati wants me to go to night school. I don't know. It might be fun to go and meet others—maybe some boys," Liisa laughed. "I don't really need English in my job. The cook tells me what to do. I hardly even see the lady of the house. But you should see the house! It's big with many, many rooms. The cook and I have a room on the third floor with our own staircase to the kitchen. There are only a Mister, and a Missus, and a Miss besides the cook, me, and a woman who comes in to clean, and the laundry woman. The

Mister is tall and wears a funny round hat. His wife is fat, the Miss is pretty and wears beautiful clothes."

"Father says you get Thursday afternoon off. What do you do when you don't have to work?" Anna was curious.

"So far I've just gone to Saimi-tati's or to the stores but just yesterday I met a girl from Finland who works in the next house. She's only a couple of years older than I am and she came over here all by herself. She goes to the hall to see plays and to dances. She invited me to go with her. That will be exciting."

"Mother and Father won't let you," Anna said.

"I'm a grown up now, earning my own money," Liisa straightened herself to emphasize her independence.

Anna felt uneasy. That world out there seemed to be taking Liisa away. She was sure, she, Anna would never leave home. She remembered Lillian talking about the town schools—about being pushed into a ditch because she was from Finland. And now, Lillian, her one town friend wouldn't even come to see her. Maybe Liisa was right in wanting to move back to Finland. Anna suddenly felt very lonely for her grandparents and for her aunts and uncles. She didn't even want to think that she'd never see them again.

Chapter Twenty-Three

Spring became early summer and Anna felt happy again. The leaves grew quickly from their tiny mouse-ear beginnings into lavish green coverings for the hills and valleys. The saskatoon and then the wild cherry blossomed, making Anna think of the poem in her Reader about an apple orchard. Father was busy planting the little fields he had cleared from the bush, the summer and fall before, and plowed earlier in the spring with Bobby. One day when she came home from school, Mother was moving everything back into the house after spring cleaning. The house smelled of soap and fresh air. Father had tacked cheese cloth to the lower parts of the window, so they could keep them open without the nuisance of mosquitoes. Anna woke up in the mornings to Mustikki's bell sounding rhythmically as she chewed on the patches of grass behind the barn. The days were long and they didn't need a lamp in the morning and hardly even at night. It seemed to Anna that the whole world had opened up to light and air.

At school, although talk still continued about passing, another more pleasant topic was popular—that of the school picnic. It was to be held at the school and it happened to fall on St. John's

Day, Juhannus. Some of the older pupils had wanted to have it at the lake in order to have a big bonfire as was the custom in Finland, but when the teacher found out that the lake was two miles away, over a bush trail, she was adamant about having it at school. She said she did not want to lose any of the little ones into the bush or the lake. Besides, she said, they would need the school yard for races and games. When the older girls explained to the teacher that all the grown-ups were coming too, because it was Juhannus, the teacher looked startled. She smiled nervously.

"But it's a week day. I thought they would all be working."

"Juhannus is a holiday in Finland and they like to keep that a holiday," one of the girls explained.

"They are now in Canada . . . " the teacher started saying angrily, but then softened her voice, "Of course, they will be welcome. Will they look after the food?"

The girls all said, "Yes, yes, we will all bring the food!"

Earlier in the spring Father had bought a wagon that he needed for working on the farm, but it was slow and bumpy for riding in.

One day Anna was surprised to find a buggy in the yard, when she arrived home from school. Father had been able to get one second hand at a good price.

Anna loved riding in it. She felt so grand sitting on the padded seat overlooking Bobby's back and the road ahead. The roof and the sides were of shiny black material and shaded her from the sun and the wind. It was altogether a lovely way to ride, much better than the clumsy farm wagon.

It was after they got the buggy that they decided to go into town again. They started off early, on a bright June morning right after Mother milked Mustikki.

As Bobby trotted up hill and down hill, Anna looked at the thick greenness along the roadside. Occasionally a squirrel would run across the road, or a bird would swing on a branch just above them. There would be a gate to a farmhouse and a dog would bark. As they got closer into town, there were more farms and fields. Anna was pleased to see daisies and buttercups along the roadsides. When they reached the top of the hill above the town, she could see the small mountain in the distance and the Giant, the big rock that looked like a man lying across the bay, and Lake Superior shining blue and sparkling.

But just as they got into the outskirts of the town, a strange thing happened. A carriage without a horse and making a great noise came towards them. Bobby became frightened and started to pull them off the road and to rise up on his hind legs.

Mother cried out, "Voi, voi," and hung tightly to Anna. Father tried to calm Bobby by talking to him and pulling on the reins. He finally had to get out and stand by Bobby's head, patting and soothing him.

Mother and Anna sat in the buggy clutching each other.

Finally Father was able to quieten him, some time after the machine had passed.

"That's an automobile," Mother said, as she let go of Anna. "Do you remember the one in Kotka? One of the sawmill bosses had one. I hope there aren't too many in town or we might have worse trouble with Bobby. Horses sometimes go completely wild."

"They shouldn't allow those things on the roads," Father grumbled as he climbed back up beside them.

"Maybe we should leave the horse at Perttula's, instead of going down to the main street with him. We can always take the street car down."

"I don't know. I don't think there are that many automobiles here, I don't know, maybe you're right."

"We have to stop there anyway with the milk and the cream. Let's ask," Mother suggested.

Bobby was safely settled in Perttula's backyard and Anna, Mother, Father, Saimi-tati, and Lillian were sitting in the street-car on their way downtown. Anna enjoyed the feel of the wicker seat, and the rhythmic swaying of the street car.

Mother wanted to visit Liisa and so Saimi-tati came along to show them the way. Also, since Saimi-tati had worked for the same people and knew the cook, it would be easier to go with her to the big house. Lillian was friendly again and told Anna about school, socials, but especially about her Canadian girl friend.

"She's my best friend now, she comes to my house all the time," she declared.

As they got off the street car on the main street, Father left them to do business, while Anna, Mother, Saimi-tati, and Lillian all got on another streetcar to go where Liisa was working. They were to meet Father later at Perttula's.

Anna looked in wonder at the big houses on the street where Liisa worked. They were tall and had many windows, balconies, and decorations. When they got to Liisa's work place, they did not go in from the big front door but to the back where an ordinary door opened into the kitchen.

The cook was a friendly woman who teased Anna and Lillian and called them mademoiselles. Liisa looked different in her black dress, funny little white bonnet, and white frilly apron. She looked shy and Anna felt that she was not really glad to see them.

"Please sit down at the table. I'll give you a cup of coffee and a piece of cake. The lady of the house is out for the day," the cook said.

Anna had the feeling that they were doing something wrong and that soon the lady of the house would come home and chase them all away.

"This is a good place to work," the cook was saying as they were having their coffee. "The lady of the house is very demanding, but very fair, and she pays promptly, not like some. Your daughter will do well here, as long as she does her work conscientiously. Notice her new uniform. That means that she is not just a kitchen maid but has other duties as well. As I was saying, as long as she does her work well. But," she lowered her voice, "I'm not sure that that servant next door will be a good influence. She goes to the Hall too much, and is much too independent."

Liisa blushed bright red at these words.

Anna expected Mother to question the cook, but she said nothing, just looked uncomfortable. But when they got outside, she demanded from Saimi-tati, "what did that cook mean? Has Liisa been running around? If she starts that sort of thing, she better come home."

"Come Eeva, you don't expect her to just work and not have any fun. We go to the Hall and we have seen her there a couple of times and she conducts herself very well. I don't think you have to worry about her. That cook doesn't go anywhere, just works and that isn't good."

Saimi-tati's words didn't seem to comfort Mother very much. "She is so young and headstrong and I'm afraid for her. I often wonder if it was right to come to this country. It will be much harder for her."

"Hah, I was only a little older, when I came all by myself and I got along fine," Saimi-tati said.

Mother just sighed and said nothing.

Anna looked back at the house and she wished she could have seen the rest of it and not just the kitchen. It was many times finer than Lillian's.

Lillian hadn't said anything at all when they were inside but out on the street she told Anna that her Canadian friend's house was very much the same. "I have eaten in their dining room many times, served by a girl in a uniform like Liisa's," she boasted.

They got back on the streetcar. Anna liked the rumbling sound it made, and it seemed to go so fast—the houses just flashed by.

At one of the stops Lillian poked Anna excitedly. "There's my friend, my Canadian friend. She's with her cousins. I have met them too." Then she lowered her voice and said, "they're really stuck-up, I don't like them much. I wish your mother and my mother didn't talk so loud in Finn."

The three girls Lillian pointed to were very pretty and were dressed in stylish clothes.

"The girl in green is my friend," Lillian whispered.

As the three approached them along the aisle, the two cousins stared at Mother and Saimi-tati as if they were some kind of repulsive creatures. Lillian's friend smiled and said hello, but the other two pulled her away impatiently. "You shouldn't talk to foreigners," the older one said. Then Anna heard the other one say, "They shouldn't be allowed to talk in that crazy language in public places. Don't they know they are in Canada? My mother says your mother is crazy to let you be friends with that girl."

Anna was afraid to look at Lillian. She knew how terrible those words must be to her.

When they got to the main street, Mother asked Saimi-tati if Lillian could come with them instead of going home with her. Anna was glad. Maybe that might cheer her up a little; she looked so sad.

And they did have a good time, in spite of everything. Mother brought them an ice cream cone, and they walked up and down the main street. They went in and out of the stores and laughed and talked. Mother bought some cups and saucers.

"We don't have enough for when company comes," she said.

But what pleased Anna was the pink gingham dress material Mother bought her. "You are growing out of your summer clothes, and I hate to cut down Liisa's old ones for you. You can wear those when you grow into them. This is on sale. I think I can afford it. Maybe I'll even get it sewn for the school picnic."

Saimi-tati had given Lillian some money. She wanted to get beads and so she and Anna pondered a long time at the dime store jewelry counter. Finally Lillian chose a string of black beads. Mother protested, "Aren't those a little old for you?"

But Lillian just said, "I like them and many of the girls at school have the same kind."

Father was already at Perttula's when they got back. Saimi-tati had a meal ready for them after which they left for home.

Anna slept most of the way against Mother's shoulder.

She woke up as they were climbing their own lane. The western sky was a clear lemon yellow against which the spruce tops made a series of patterns. Along the lane the green branches of bushes and trees stretched out to them in a friendly way, it seemed to Anna. There was a smell of growing things, and the brook below the hill was loud in its early summer rush of water, competing with the chanting of the frogs.

Anna knew that this was home. Lillian's girl-friend's cousins couldn't take this away from her.

Chapter Twenty-Four

One Friday when Anna got home from school she found Mother in tears and even Father looked very depressed.

"What is the matter?" Anna asked Mother. "What's happened?" She was afraid something had happened to Liisa.

"Young Helvi Maki died last night. Poor, poor Jussi—he is all alone and he is so young." Mother's tears started flowing again. "I've asked him to come to stay here over night. I don't know if he will, but if he does, you'll have to sleep in our room."

"What happened? I just saw her yesterday and she wasn't sick."

"I can't talk about it. She's been very lonely and homesick, but I didn't think it was that bad. We should have done more for her. She was so young and so far from other relatives." Mother turned away and Anna knew she was crying again.

After what seemed a long while to Anna, Mother wiped her eyes and shook herself into action. "We have much to do. The funeral is tomorrow. Korpi has gone into town to get the pastor. Helmi's mother, Korpi-tati, and some of the other women are getting together to prepare coffee for the funeral at the school. She will be buried near the only other grave in this community,

Mrs. Ranta's grave, on the Ranta land across from the school. We have to be Jussi's family. I promised to make a couple of cakes and some sandwiches. You can help me with the sandwiches."

Maki-seta came later in the evening. He was a tall man with dark eyes and dark hair. He was stooped over and hardly looked at any of them. He just mumbled "Kiitos" when Mother offered him coffee. He drank his coffee in silence and then went straight to bed.

Anna felt as if there were a heavy black cloud hanging over the house. She thought and thought about what could have happened. Then she began to feel sorry for the young woman lying in the coffin her husband had made for her. Anna was glad she was sleeping in the same room with Mother and Father.

In the morning Maki-seta was gone by the time Anna woke up. Mother said he went home to make preparations to take the coffin to the schoolhouse for the service in the afternoon.

"We have to take the wagon today. We have too much to take to the schoolhouse—cakes, sandwiches, dishes—to fit into the buggy."

Anna helped Mother with packing the boxes and bags, carrying them into the wagon. On one of their trips outside they heard wagon wheels on the road. They stopped to look down to the edge of the clearing where the road was visible. Soon they saw Maki-seta, and his horse and wagon. He was sitting on the seat in the front with the coffin behind him. Both Anna and her mother just stood there. Anna could see her Mother's face twisting into a silent sob. They watched until he was out of sight.

"She was so young. Homesickness is a terrible thing," Mother said as they turned to go inside.

When they arrived at the school, some men were setting up a table on the shady side of the building. Some of the other women were already there with their donations.

"There isn't enough room inside," one of the women told Mother. "If we leave everything covered up it should be alright. Set the cups and saucers up-side-down."

Mother and Korpi-tati took out their white linen cloths and started setting the table.

In the middle of the school yard a fire was burning between some stones and a large pot full of water was being readied for coffee making.

The school room looked strange to Anna. The desks were arranged across the room as if they were pews and there were extra benches set up behind them. The coffin rested on boards supported by trestles in front of the teacher's desk. The pastor was already there in his black coat and winged collar and Maki-seta sat humped down in the front seat. Anna watched the people filing in quietly. The women wore dark dresses and most of the men were in dark clothes, some in Sunday suits, and others in dark trousers and sweaters. To Anna, as she sat between Father and Mother, the thing seemed to fit together—the dark clothes, the quietness, the coffin, and when the first hymn started, its slow melancholy tune became part of the same somberness. Anna pondered over the words of the sermon, Helvi-tati was like a seed that was put into the ground, and she would come alive in the resurrection.

After the last hymn was sung everyone passed by the coffin quietly. Anna thought that Helmi-tati looked as if she were sleeping. When everyone had gone by the coffin, Father and Korpi-seta took the wooden cover from the corner, laid it over the coffin and hammered it closed. Maki-seta was still sitting and to Anna it seemed that his shoulders jerked every time a hammer hit a nail.

Then four other men joined Father and Korpi-seta to carry the coffin to the little cemetery across the road. Maki-seta at first did not move, not until Mother went over and took him by the arm and led him after the coffin. There was an open grave among the trees. The men had two ropes with which they lowered the coffin into the grave. Anna felt the solemnity of the moment, especially when the pastor intoned, "Dust to dust . . . " as he dropped loose earth on the coffin. When he prayed, Anna could hear only the sound of his voice but she did not know what he was saying. Another hymn was sung and then some of the men began to fill in the grave. The rest of the people walked back to the school, and suddenly everyone was talking again.

Mother, Korpi-tati, Helmi's mother and some of the other women started to take the covers off the cakes and sandwiches, to fetch coffee in their coffee pots from the big pot on the fire. Mother saw to it that Maki-seta sat down first and then the others joined him.

When Anna got back home, she wandered around the homestead, feeling sad and lonely. She went to her favorite places but these did not seem to help. She found a dead bird near the hayloft. She ran inside and into her room to get a pretty box Lillian had given her. She lifted the bird with two sticks into the box, put the cover on and then got Father's spade, dug a hole near one of the play rocks and buried the box. But before she covered it she said all she could of the funeral service; she even tried to sing a hymn. As she covered the box, she felt much better.

Chapter Twenty-Five

The days continued warm and it was difficult to sit in the schoolroom when there were so many things to do outside.

At noon hour and recesses, talk was mostly about the coming picnic. It was turning out to be a big community gathering. Mother even had a letter from Liisa saying that she and some young people were planning on hiring a horse and coming out for it.

"I wonder what kind of people she is taking up with," Mother said, "I hope they're a decent sort."

"There's nothing we can do about it now, but it seems to me that if they want to come to a country picnic they can't be that bad," Father comforted.

"I'd still feel better if she were coming with Saimi and Kalle. She is so young," Mother still looked worried.

"Well, at least there's one thing we can be happy about. She's no longer talking about going back to the Old Country," Father said.

The day before the picnic was beautiful day. Anna met Helmi at the end of the lane. They dawdled, picking strawberries from the roadside and blowing dandelion heads. They forgot about time until they heard the school bell and they were still below the school hill.

They were hot and out of breath when they got inside the door. The teacher hadn't started the opening prayer and reading yet and she waited for them to sit down.

"Where were you two?" She asked, but she did not seem to be angry.

After they finished the arithmetic exercise, the teacher asked them to open their Readers. Both Anna and Helmi worried that they wouldn't have time to finish the First Reader and so not be able to start the Second Reader in the fall.

"Slow down, Anna," the teacher said. "You sound as if you were racing somewhere. You haven't time to think about all the pretty things mentioned in this poem. Start again at 'and buttercups are coming, and scarlet columbine, And in the sunny meadows, The dandelions shine'. Now try it, much more slowly and with emphasis."

Anna tried again.

"That's better, but you are still hurrying. But we haven't time to do it again."

Anna's heart sank. Would that mean that she wouldn't get into the Second Reader? But the teacher continued, "We won't worry about it now. The main thing is that you are able to read it. You can read the rest of the pieces to yourselves while I hear the Second and Third classes. I must tell you that you both have done very well this year. I hope you keep it up when you get into the Second Reader." The teacher smiled at them.

Anna's heart lifted with happiness. Next fall she would not be in a baby class anymore. It amused her to remember that just a year ago she thought that English had no words.

In the afternoon they cleaned out their desks and when everything was done the teacher had them sit with the work books, text books, and pencil boxes neatly piled up in front of them. The teacher's desk was clear except for a pile of report cards.

She started by giving the Primary cards first. Anna could feel herself stiffen as her turn came closer. She still worried in spite of the teacher's earlier encouragement. When her turn came, she had difficulty getting out of her desk, and on the way to the teacher's desk she almost tripped on the platform. She got back to her desk somehow and opened the report card. Now she knew she passed for sure, and her marks were good. She grinned at Helmi and Helmi grinned at her because she too was happy with her report.

Anna was startled to hear Aarne's low, rumbling swearing in Finnish from the row of big desks.

"I beg your pardon, Aarne?" the teacher said. "I warned you many times. You just did not do the work."

"I don't care, I don't care. I wasn't going to come back in the fall anyway," he said in a loud voice.

"Silence, please. Let us close with prayer," the teacher commanded.

Anna could still hear mutterings from the big boys' desks. She almost felt sorry for Aarne. He was so big he could hardly fit into his desk. Because of his size he had been the boss of the school, but now he was the only one who did not pass.

After school dismissed, they milled around the steps for a few minutes comparing report cards. Aarne strode from group to group talking loudly. Every time he passed Anna and Helmi he reached out to flick his fingers at their heads—"Old Country dumbbells," he chanted. But the girls just laughed as they dodged his fingers.

Chapter Twenty-Six

The picnic day started out threatening rain, and Anna worried. But as the time came closer, the clouds dispersed and by the time they climbed into the buggy the sky was cloudless.

"This is a perfect Juhannus Day, like the days I remember from my childhood," Father said.

Mother laughed, "Isn't it funny how we always remember the nice days. That's how I remember the Old Country, the sun always shining."

Anna tried to remember Finland. She could see the street they lived on and she could remember Mummo's farm. But there was so much she had already forgotten.

As they neared the schoolhouse, there were other wagons and buggies coming from various directions and many people were already in the school yard. The women were clustered, talking under the birch trees where a table was set up. Some of the men were standing by the steps smoking. A few of the younger men were setting up for the sports—posts for the high jump, preparing a patch of ground for the long jumps, measuring for the races. It looked to Anna that Olavi's father was in charge. Anna couldn't see the teacher anywhere—maybe she was in her own place at the back of the school. *She wouldn't be able to understand anything*, Anna thought. Everyone, even the school children were all speaking Finnish.

Anna and Helmi wandered from one group to another. They looked at the sandwiches and cakes.

"I hope we eat soon," Helmi said.

"So do I. I'm hungry," Anna agreed.

They went to where the big pot was over the fire, as it had been at Helmi-tati's funeral.

"When it boils, maybe we'll eat," Anna supposed.

But just then Olavi's father called all the school children together by the school steps, where he explained about the races for the different age groups. At that moment the teacher came out with a handful of ribbons. She was going to hand them to Olavi's father, but he, with his few words of English and hand gestures made her understand that she should give the ribbons to the winners. Anna noticed that the teacher's face became pink and she was smiling.

The races were fun. She and Helmi came first and second in two of the shorter runs and Helmi won the high jump for their age group. They were all hot and sweaty when the word went out that lunch was served. They hurried to the tables, but Anna's mother made them go into the schoolhouse to wash their hands. "You can't eat with hands like that. Go on, there's lots of food, you won't be left without."

While they were eating Anna suddenly remembered that Liisa was supposed to come. Maybe she couldn't get away from her work place. Anna was disappointed.

"Where's everyone going?" Helmi's mother said, shortly after they had finished eating. The picnickers were moving out of the gate towards the road.

Helmi and Anna pushed their way, ahead of the others. A carriage with a team of horses was stopped by the side of the road.

Helmi said, "It's your sister."

Anna stared at Liisa. She looked so different. She was dressed in a navy blue suit with a white frilly blouse and a navy hat full of daisies. She looked so grown-up and pretty.

Liisa laughed, "Anna, why are you staring at me like that? Aren't you going to greet your sister?"

Without thinking, she curtsied as she had been taught in Finland even though no one did it here anymore.

"What a funny little sister," Liisa said as she leaned over to hug her.

Liisa had descended from the front seat and the man who drove the horses came around and stood by Liisa. He was just a little taller than Liisa; he had light brown hair and blue eyes.

"Matti, this my little sister, Anna," Liisa turned Anna to face Matti.

Again Anna curtsied, but then felt embarrassed. Matti smiled and put out his hand, "Good day, Anna. I'm glad to meet Liisa's little sister."

By this time the other couple had come down from the back seat of the carriage.

"Elvi and Veikko, this is my little sister, Anna."

"Good day," they both said and shook hands with her.

Anna wasn't sure she wanted to be introduced as "little," but she liked the way they shook hands with her.

By this time Mother and Father had reached the roadside. After the introductions Mother urged them to come and eat lunch and have some coffee.

"We'll have our lunch first," Liisa turned to Matti, "And then we'll bring out the treat."

"What treat?" Mother wanted to know. But Liisa and her friends just laughed.

"You'll have to wait," she said.

The visitors made quite a stir. Liisa's friend, Matti, was talkative and he was soon chatting with Father and the other men.

Liisa played with Korpi's little boy and marvelled how much he had grown in the few months she had been away.

Anna was pleased to see that the older girls gathered around too, and stared at Liisa and her friends. It made Anna feel important to have Liisa looking so nice. But the real excitement started when Matti and Veikko carried a large wooden container to the table. Everyone gathered around to see what was going on.

"I know what it is! It's ice cream," somebody shouted.

Matti made all kinds of funny comments as he opened the big container and then another one inside the large one packed in ice. He began to fill cones, handing them out first to the smallest children, then Anna and Helmi got theirs. Matti teased Anna that he made hers bigger than the rest.

Anna thought the ice cream tasted better than the one she had had in town—maybe it was because she had not expected ice cream at the school picnic.

When everyone was served, Olavi's father climbed up on the school steps and began to make a speech.

"My good neighbors, visitors and teacher," He bowed slightly towards her. "This has been a great Juhannus celebration, maybe not quite how we remember it from the Old Country, but still pretty good. It shows that we can make a place for ourselves in this new land, among the birches and pines of Canada. We all have our memories from the Old Country which we will never forget, but our future is here. This little schoolhouse is the beginning of us becoming Canadians—at least our children will be part of this new land. Let's give a loud hurrah for our new home."

Loud cheers went up from the crowd. The pupils enjoyed making a great noise. The grown-ups had difficulty calming them down after that.

Anna could see one of the older girls explaining what was going on to the teacher. The teacher smiled and Anna saw her wipe her eyes with her handkerchief.

Then everything was over. The women began to pack up the remains of the lunch, and the plates and the dishes they had brought. The men put out the fire under the coffee pot and took down the trestle table to store it under the school building.

Mother asked Liisa and her friends if they had time to come back with them.

"What do you think?" Liisa asked Matti.

"Voi, voi, I would like to, but it's too late, we have to get the horses back for seven o'clock, and it will take us a couple of hours to get back."

"That's too bad," Mother said.

"We will come back some time when Liisa gets a day off," Matti shook hands with Mother and Father.

"I'm sorry they couldn't come home with us. Maybe we could have found out more about him," Mother said as they were riding homeward. "I'm so worried because she's so young and I've heard so many stories about these men coming over here and pretending they're single, when they have wife and children in the Old Country. I think I will write to Saimi and ask her to look into it."

"I suppose that won't hurt, if she goes about it quietly and doesn't make a big fuss," Father said.

"Yes, that's what I'll do," Mother said and then added, "he certainly is friendly and talkative. Maybe a little too talkative for a man."

Anna felt vaguely uncomfortable, listening to her Mother's worries. it had been such a wonderful day—winning the race, good things to eat, especially the ice cream and best of all seeing Liisa and her friends. She felt warm and safe just being there among the people who lived in the same community. But now this worry that something bad might happen to Liisa crept inside her head and made her feel uneasy and anxious.

Chapter Twenty-Seven

The long, warm, summer days made Anna forget her worries. She walked down to the creek below the hill to watch the fish swimming about. She played with her pretend cows and chickens under the big pine tree. Once in awhile, Helmi came over and they played house on the big rocks, or she and Mother went over to Helmi's for a visit. Other times, she helped Mother feed the chickens and sometimes to get Mustikki when she strayed too far into the woods behind the pasture. All her favorite places were now so familiar, that Anna felt as if she had always lived on the homestead. It was hard to believe that they had been there only a little more than a year.

Saimi-tati's letter, in answer to Mother's questions about Matti came one day. Anna tried to figure out from Mother's face if the news was bad or good. She couldn't really tell which it was. At first Mother smiled a little, but by the time she finished the letter there were tears in her eyes.

Anna knew that it would be no use asking Mother; she would just say, "you are too young to think about these things." She would have to wait until Father came in and be around when they talked about it.

She had to wait until supper time.

"Did you read Saimi's letter?" Mother asked Father.

"Yes, well—it's good news isn't it? She has it from reliable sources, from someone who comes from the same parish, that at least he's not married and as far as she knows he's got a good reputation of being a good worker."

"Yes, I know that's good, but she also says it looks serious. It's all happening too fast and she's too young. She doesn't know what she is doing. Besides she should have said something to us," Mother was upset.

"Well, yes, she certainly should talk to us before she does anything. As for age, can you remember how old you were when we got engaged?" Father had a funny smile on his face.

"That was different," Mother said.

"How different?" Father asked.

"I was much more serious than she is, for one thing. We were part of the same community. I had known you all my life. Anyway, let's not talk about that."

"Is Liisa getting married?" Anna asked.

"You do have long ears, don't you, my little one," Mother looked at her. "Yes, it seems that according to Saimi-tati it might happen."

"Don't call me little. I'm not little anymore," Anna complained, then added, "then Liisa won't be going back to Finland, will she?"

"No, I guess not," Mother said.

The next mail day they had a letter from Liisa, in which she said that she and Matti were coming the following Sunday.

"That's tomorrow already. Good heavens," Mother exclaimed. "I must get some baking done."

Anna was glad they were coming so soon. She could not have stood waiting for many days. Now she just had to wait over night.

Liisa had the same clothes on that she had at the school picnic. She was smiling and happy and she brought presents for everyone. Anna got a fancy pencil box, Mother a shiny table cloth with fringes, and Father a summer shirt.

"You shouldn't spend your small salary on us," Mother protested, but seemed pleased at the same time.

Matti was quieter than he had been at the picnic.

Father and he walked around the homestead. Anna wanted to follow, but Mother called her to come inside with her and Liisa.

Mother made some coffee and set the table. It was strange to have Liisa acting like a visitor. She had grown so far from Anna. They used to have such fun together when they were in Finland, playing house and playing games. Now she and Mother talked like two women. Anna felt sad, but yet in a funny way proud of this new sister.

"When do you plan on getting married?" Mother asked.

"Oh, not for awhile yet. We want to earn money. I'll keep working so together we can maybe earn enough for a house."

"In town?" Mother looked surprised.

"Of course. Matti works on the street car tracks, the same place where Kalle-seta works. And even when we're married I'll work like Saimi-tati does."

"That's good. Yes, I sometimes wish that your father wouldn't have such a love for land. He hated living in Kotka. That's when he started dreaming about land here. I take it that you are no longer planning on going back to Finland," Mother's voice sounded teasing.

"No, I guess not."

Just then Father and Matti came in. Father was in a talkative mood. *He must like Matti*, Anna decided.

In Anna's opinion the visit went too quickly; she hated to see them leave.

"It looks as if we are putting down more than one root into this country," Father said as they watched the horse and buggy going down the lane.

Anna didn't know what Father meant, but she was happy. She had the rest of the summer before her and when school started in the fall she would be in second class and not in a baby class anymore.

Just as they turned to go back into the house Father stopped, and pointed towards the gate. "There's someone walking up our lane," He said and added, "It's a stranger." They stood and waited.

A man trudged up the lane burdened down by a large pack.

"It's some kind of pedlar," Mother said, as she turned to open the door.

"Don't go in lady," the man called, as he hurried towards them. "I have something for your kitchen."

The pedlar set down his pack, opened it, and began to lay out his wares on the step in front of them. "Spices and flavorings for you." He looked at Mother and pointed to tins and jars. "And for you, sir, I have wagon grease and all kinds of medicines for animals and people."

Mother bought a tin of cinnamon, and Father a bottle of liniment. Then Mother said in Finnish, "Poor man, he looks tired, and no wonder, carrying that pack such long distances. Anna, ask him to come in." When Anna relayed the invitation, his face brightened, and Anna noticed how young he looked when he smiled. He turned to Mother and repeated, "Thank you, thank you, thank you very much."

He had three cups of coffee and several pieces of pulla. He smiled at Anna and asked her about school and about her summer. Anna was surprised that she didn't feel shy. She told him about her report card and what class she would be in September and even about some of the books she had read. She was surprised because she had never before spoken to an adult, except the teacher, in English.

After the man heaved his pack on his back, thanked Mother many times and left, Father put his hand on Anna's shoulder and said, "I see that I now have my own interpreter, when I go to some business place in town. I won't have to find someone to interpret for me!"

Anna felt warm and happy, and she wondered how she could ever have thought that English had no words.

About the Author

Elizabeth Kouhi was born in a small pioneer community near Thunder Bay, Ontario. Her education proceeded in fits and starts from a one-room school house, to graduation from McGill University in Montreal in 1949, and a teaching diploma from the Ontario College of Education in Toronto in 1964. She taught in a one-room school house and then in a high school for nineteen years, retiring in 1982. She is married with four children and ten grandchildren. She lives in Thunder Bay, Ontario, where she writes books for children and poetry.